THE SPIDER:
THE MAN WHO RULED IN HELL

MASTER OF MEN!

THE SPIDER®

THE MAN WHO RULED IN HELL

By Grant Stockbridge

STEEGER BOOKS • 2021

CHAPTER 1
THE RED HAND

THE HEADWAITER spoke softly into Richard Wentworth's ear, and Wentworth's lids dropped to hide the abruptly sharpened gleam of his eyes. He leaned toward the girl beside him, lips still smiling.

"Just a phone call, Nita," he whispered, and rose to make apologies to his other guests. But it was on Nita van Sloan that his gaze lingered. He saw her violet eyes darken, saw now her slim hands clenched stiffly in her lap.

Her lips formed a single questioning word, "Laskar?"

Wentworth shrugged as he bowed and left—but he knew! Laskar had tried to reach him earlier in the evening and Wentworth's call back had gone unanswered—until now. Yes, it would be Laskar. Ben Laskar, to whom Wentworth had imparted the secret that could destroy them both overnight! That Wentworth was in truth—the Spider!

Laskar was proud to share that perilous secret; proud, too, to be the Spider's contact man with the world at large. Many of the oppressed and needy had come to Laskar crying out for protection from crooks too canny for the law to snare; for justice against ruthless and untouchable overlords of crime. And the Spider, deadly swift nemesis of all who lived outside the law, had never failed them—would never fail them, please God!

Wentworth's blue-gray eyes were alert as, under lowered lids,

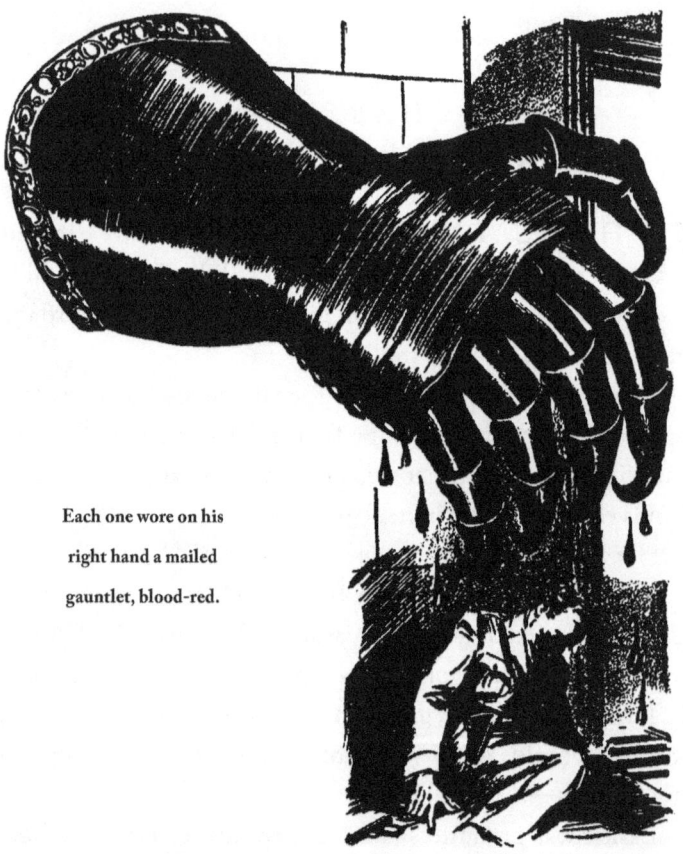

Each one wore on his
right hand a mailed
gauntlet, blood-red.

they swept the corridors through which he strode beside the
headwaiter. There was another danger. Criminals, too, had used
Laskar to set traps for the man they hated, whose swift, impar-
tial justice they feared more than all the minions of the law!
But the halls seemed without menace as Wentworth entered
the phone booth.

"Richard Wentworth speaking," he said quietly, then his fist closed hard and white about the phone. "Louder, Laskar," he urged. "What's the matter with you, man? Are you hurt?" He ground the earpiece closer to his head. "All right, Laskar. Hold on. Hold hard! I'll be there in five minutes!"

He spun from the booth—and Nita van Sloan's hands clutched at his lapels. Just for a moment, then she stepped back and stood with a stiff smile on her lips, while that fear lay darkly in her eyes.

"Trouble, Dick?" she asked quietly.

Wentworth took her slim white hands in his. So, Nita, too, had guessed that this call might summon Wentworth once more to don the dark, perilous garments of the Spider! Yes, she shared his secret, too. Their love gave her that right, as her love now had sensed danger.

"Probably nothing much," Wentworth said lightly. "Laskar wants to talk with me. Make my excuses, Nita dear, to my guests. I'll be back soon." And in his heart, he added *"I hope!"*

For Laskar had been scarcely able to speak and what he had whispered over the wire meant nothing to Wentworth. *"The Red Hand! The Red Hand!"* Afterward had come no words at all, but gibbering, hoarse screams! And this was Ben Laskar, who had served the Spider so faithfully, and who, even in fierce peril, thought first to warn the man to whom he gave such loyalty!

Wentworth's deceptively easy stride carried him swiftly toward the cloak room and exit. Tall, with a flat-planed, vital face too strong to be merely handsome, Wentworth was a man who drew people's eyes everywhere. Evening dress seemed to have been created expressly to set off his flat-backed, athletic figure. His shoulders had a quietly confident swing, and there was an almost arrogant poise to the modeled head capped in crisp black hair. Here was a man to command, such a one as might in troublous times rise spontaneously to kingship—a master of men. Wentworth chose to serve, selflessly.

Now, once more, the service Wentworth elected had brought injury, perhaps death, to a loyal comrade! Laskar had been suffering terribly. His voice left no doubt of that....

The outer doors of the Waldorf were whipped open before Wentworth's lengthening stride. A taxi driver broke a half dozen regulations in a race for Laskar's off-Broadway office. Wentworth was out of the cab before it stopped, and across the sidewalk in a bound. Even so, his keen gaze scanned the street. At Eighth Avenue, two taxis waited for a green light. A drunk lay asleep in the doorway of an unused theater, and against Broadway's glow, a mounted policeman made an equestrian statue in black. That was all, but... Was that thin, high whistle he could just hear a signal of some kind? No time to see. Upstairs was Laskar....

THE EMPTY third floor corridor echoed to Wentworth's impatient tread. His right hand slid deftly beneath the silken lapel of his coat, and his pace increased. A stride from Laskar's door, he lifted his right foot and smashed the heel against the lock. It shattered. The door rocketed inward. Wentworth dodged through the opening in a gliding sideways leap—and stood motionless, wordless. The office was wrecked. Only one chair still stood upright in the middle of the room. And beside it, on the floor....

Even as he dropped to his knees beside the tossing body of Ben Laskar, Wentworth's eyes flicked over the office, darted to the lone airshaft window. His breath sucked in. As his knees hit, Wentworth ducked, lunged forward. Something struck his silk hat with a note curiously like a broken drumhead. The hat lifted from his head, and Wentworth grunted as chest and head slammed against the floor. It was only then that he heard the machine gun hammer in the airshaft.

Wentworth rolled to the left, sent the upright chair skittering, came up on his knees breasting the outer wall. He thrust his gun hand through the window and in a swift drum-roll of fire, fanned out six swift shots that were swallowed up in the heavier blasts of the machine gun. The racket stopped so abruptly that Wentworth's ears ached. He heard the chair he had hit slam to the floor in a ricochet off the wall, heard his own quick breath. Behind him, Ben Laskar made a moaning noise.

Wentworth's eyes held a hard glitter as he looked at his light automatic, the thirty-two he carried when he wore evening dress. One shot left. One shot… His right sleeve was ripped by machine-gun slugs. His lips twitched. He caught up the chair, threw his coat across its back, crawled across under the window before he drew the shoulder of the coat slowly into sight. When the machine gun blasted out again, Wentworth took his chance, a quick glance over the sill on the opposite side of the window to guide his one shot.

Twenty feet away across the airshaft, the machine gunner stood to handle his weapon. He was crouched over it, his face, twisted in a hard grin, clearly visible in the reflection of his gun's flickering powder-flame. His first burst caught the coat shoulder, hammered it backward with the chair. Wentworth could

even see the man's eyes widen, his
grin stiffen on his lips as he realized
he had been tricked; saw his hands
fighting the recoil to bring the gun
about—too late.

Wentworth's slug threw a little to
the left. It took the man in the left eye
instead of the forehead.

Wentworth watched him collapse, then he wheeled to kneel
again beside Laskar. His movements lost none of their crispness,
but his hands were very gentle as he turned his comrade over.
Then a queer tortured curse forced itself out between Wentworth's suddenly locked teeth. Good God, *what had they done
to Laskar's face!*

By some miracle, Wentworth kept his own countenance
impassive, for Laskar's eyes were on his. Devoted, loyal eyes even
now when the man was dying. Laskar tried to lift a clenched
fist, to push out words, but the hand seemed powerless and his
words were without form, horrible. Foam worked out between
his champing teeth. His back arched and his jaws yawned in a
soundless scream. Wentworth's arms, closed hard about him, felt
the last quiver when life left—and he was glad! Laskar would
not want to live with a face like that!

With flinching eyes, Wentworth forced himself then to
look again on his murdered comrade. Across mouth and jaws,
some hideous device of torture had clamped. And where it had
touched, the incredible pure white of the bone and the clenched
teeth were exposed! Every vestige of flesh had been stripped

off as cleanly as though the bone had been surgically scraped. It looked….

A hoarse cry forced itself from Wentworth's lips. Why, good God, that horrible disfigurement was shaped—*like a hand!* As if some monster's hand had clamped down across Laskar's mouth and cheeks, thumb and fingers gouging deep. And when it had been removed, the flesh was torn away from the bone! A hand… *The Red Hand!*

WENTWORTH'S FIRM lips twisted awry. His was the blame for this! He had killed Laskar as surely as if his own hand… A strong shudder jerked at his muscles. No wonder Laskar, over the phone, had cried, "The Red Hand!" and afterward *screamed.* Wentworth whipped to his feet, stood with drained, rigid face. This, he knew, was not an end, but an ominous beginning!

Laskar had been maimed to the sole end that, crazed with pain and fear, he would call the Spider into a machine-gun trap. And when criminals struck at the Spider, it meant a new dynasty was building in the underworld; it meant some dread and powerful being was rising to menace humanity. No lesser force would dare thus openly to challenge the swift and deadly vengeance of the Spider!

The rasp of shoe leather in the hallway whipped Wentworth about—to stare into the black eye of a revolver held by the mounted policeman Wentworth had noticed on the street.

"Hoist them," the cop said harshly. "Damn you, put them up and keep them there."

Wentworth's mind snapped out of the lethargy of pain. He

could not afford to be identified with Laskar, who was known as the contact man of the Spider. If he were forced to go to headquarters and explain his presence here, there would be more than the killing of the machine gunner to wipe out. The Spider fought on the side of law and order, but he held no law sacred if it stood in the way of his justice. So there were many warrants, many rewards for his capture—and the end of such a trail was the electric chair.

"Ben Laskar has been killed," Wentworth said sternly. He flung out a pointing hand. "Look!"

Such was the force of that command that the cop's eyes involuntarily swerved; and what he saw, the mutilation of Laskar's poor face, momentarily paralyzed him. Wentworth's punch had the force of his step-in behind it. The cop slumped into his arms. But he would not be out for long. Ten minutes at the most, and before that time Wentworth must be gone. His movements became brisk, purposeful. A wall panel opened to his secret touch and he took a fresh coat and hat from racks of clothing hung there. He knelt once more beside Laskar and drove himself, still-faced, to search the body. Clenched in a knotted fist, he found a square of paper. He gave it no more than a glance, but as he went about the rest of his brief business, his lips moved in silent curses. For on that paper was a typewritten message and a signature—the signature was *a mailed and bloody fist!*

Wentworth made a bundle of the bullet-torn hat and coat, then crossed to the desk, whipped open a drawer. A frown contracted his forehead and he picked up the single heavy automatic that lay there, swiftly discarded its ammunition and broke out a fresh box. There should be two guns, both kept here for his need. He cast a probing glance about the wrecked office, seeking the other automatic—but already the policeman was stirring. There was no time. Thoughtfully, Wentworth caught up the man's uniform cap to carry with him. A plan was already taking form in his mind… One last look he gave to Laskar's face. Despite the hideous distortion of the hand, the face was somehow calm. Calm because his dying eyes had fallen on the man he served! Wentworth's nostrils thinned and whiteness limned his lips.

"It's all right, Ben," he whispered. "All right—"

He pivoted and strode violently out of the office. His first need was to escape the vicinity, and then—a short, harsh laugh rasped from his throat—then, vengeance! But it was more than that. If he read aright the message of this bloody mailed fist, of this sacrifice of Ben Laskar, there was an even more urgent call to arms for the Spider. He must find now the source of this new menace and destroy it before it grew too great.

Despite the imminent danger of the slowly recovering policeman, Wentworth hurriedly circled through the hallways to the office whose window opposed that of Laskar across the airshaft. It was a foolhardy thing he did, a thing he was to regret through many harassed hours and days. But this killer had struck at the Spider. By God, the Red Hand should have, at once, the Spider's answer to that challenge!

Over the body of the slain machine gunner, Wentworth stood for a long moment, realizing even then the foolhardiness of his action. Then with a low curse, he whipped a cigarette lighter from his pocket. He thumbed open the base and ground it against the dead man's forehead. When he straightened a dark splotch glimmered there in the half-light, a dread symbol of sprawling hairy legs and poison fangs, a crimson spider seal which shouted to all the world that this man the Spider had justly slain!

Already, Wentworth knew he had delayed too long. He ran swiftly from the building. Except for a few taxis racing the lights the street was again empty. But he must get away at once, before the police that the Mountie undoubtedly had summoned could arrive. And he must leave inconspicuously. People would stare at and remember a man in full evening dress who carried an obvious bundle of clothing under his arm. Yet he could not abandon the bullet-torn coat and hat. It was too easily identifiable—and it linked Richard Wentworth to the man the Spider had slain.

Something of this had been in Wentworth's mind when he had snatched the policeman's cap. The horse stood nearby, forefeet on the pavement, and Wentworth nodded with satisfaction. As he had hoped, the cop carried his slicker on the cantle. In a few seconds, garbed in the uniform cap and the slicker which he draped to hide bundle and silk hat, Wentworth was cantering toward Eighth Avenue.

He timed his arrival to cross immediately with the lights, when other traffic was moving... As he trotted across the avenue, he heard the cop on duty shout something, whether challenge or greeting he could not be sure. He waved a hand and pushed on toward Ninth Avenue into the welcome darkness of the cross street. Minutes later, in his own identity, the slicker and cap

11

left with the horse, his bundle concealed in a readily purchased suitcase, he was spinning eastward in a taxi toward the Waldorf.

Now for that paper....

Momentarily secure from pursuit, Wentworth drew out the message he had taken from Laskar's dead fist. Without greeting and signed with that hellish fist, it began abruptly:

> There's ten thousand in this for you. Go to the office of Oscar Ransome, Electra Building, at precisely midnight. Collect there a package in the name of the Red Hand. Keep the ten thousand enclosed. Destroy the papers. Fail us at your peril!

Wentworth's narrowing eyes went to his watch. Half past eleven. Yes, obviously he must keep this appointment. He had no other clue. The machine gunner he had never seen before. A slow, hard smile twisted his lips. It was quite plain that the Red Hand *wanted* him to keep the appointment. Why else had the message been left in the hand of the dying Laskar?

By God, this Red Hand planned well! If the machine-gun trap failed, here was another ready. Surely, they did not expect the Spider to walk openly into such a snare? No, that would be the last thing they could imagine the Spider doing. Underworld killers would be waiting for him in every dark corner, at every secret means of ingress—waiting with murder guns cocked. Wentworth laughed softly. His course, then, was obvious! Not the Spider, but Richard Wentworth would openly keep this midnight rendezvous with death!

SEVERAL BLOCKS from the Waldorf, Wentworth dismissed the taxi, entered a drug store phone booth and called

12

Nita. Within five minutes, his sleek Daimler limousine nosed to the curb where he waited in the darkness of a side street. Before Wentworth could stop him, the bearded Sikh who served him as chauffeur and bodyguard had sprung to the pavement to open the door, bowing, lifting cupped hands to his turbaned forehead in the graceful *salaam* of the East. Even in that simple salute, there was a homage that was almost idolatry. Yet the Sikhs are a warlike and stiff-necked race!

For a moment, Wentworth paused beside the Hindu, then his hand rested lightly on the chauffeur-guard's shoulder.

"It's war again, Ram Singh," he said briefly.

His fingers sensed the powerful roll of muscles as the Sikh straightened. Teeth flashed whitely through his thick black beard.

"*Wah, sahib!*" Ram Singh's voice rumbled deeply. "It is good! Thy servant's knife grows rusty with disuse!"

Wentworth's lips tightened. Laskar's loyalty had been like this, too! He said abruptly, "Laskar is dead. Murdered."

While the Sikh's curses growled out, Wentworth gave the suitcase to him. "Destroy this and its contents." He sprang into the back beside Nita Van Sloan, and her hands reached out to him.

"I heard!" she cried softly. "Poor Ben! Surely, somewhere, there is a reward for loyalty like his… Tell me."

Her voice was ever a lovely thing in Wentworth's ears, a low rich song. It calmed his anger and bitterness now, gave him the steady strength he needed for what lay ahead. Relaxed against the cushions as Ram Singh tooled the car swiftly downtown toward the Electra Building, Wentworth told Nita concisely all that had happened, and his interpretation.

"This Oscar Ransome, to whose office Laskar was ordered," he went on, "is the lawyer who is defending Michael Taug against the government's racket charges. For once, the government seems to have slipped up. Ransome has every reason to expect to get Taug off. I don't know what the tie-up is there."

"You're keeping the appointment," Nita said quietly. "What do you want me to do?"

Wentworth felt his heart swell within him. Well he knew how Nita hated these ceaseless warrings and their perils to him, dreaded those nights when the Spider must walk again. But there was this power in her: she understood that injustice, wherever it struck, was like a pain in him which must be eased by the Spider's swift redress; it was his calling and she would not have him be untrue to himself. Wentworth drew Nita into his arms.

"What do I want you to do? Guard yourself, dearest! You are so precious to me…" He kissed her, then spoke softly. "This, Nita, is what you must do…" he said.

He sent her by taxi to the apartment building which he owned and had erected as a fortress against his never-resting enemies. She would be protected there. He knew how she longed to share his peril and doubly appreciated her unprotesting obedience.

"You'll phone… soon?" was all she said.

Then Wentworth flung himself into his preparations, changing swiftly to the dark, perfectly cut tweeds he favored, a soft felt hat from the secret wardrobe behind the rear seat. Twin forty-five caliber automatics slid into underarm clips and, as the Daimler slid to the curb before the Electra Building, he was ready.

"Wait, Ram Singh," he ordered. "If trouble starts, stand clear unless I order otherwise. And guard the *missie sahib* in all things to come with your life!" Ram Singh's *salaam* was stiff with his eagerness for battle. His *"Han, sahib!"* was a curse and a pledge.

For a moment, Wentworth stood beside him there on the curb, two fighting men together. Then Wentworth paced deliberately toward the entrance of the Electra Building, walking with quiet readiness into the Red Hand's death trap.

CHAPTER 2
WENTWORTH'S MISTAKE

THE PASSAGE into the trap was too easy. Wentworth recognized that, even as he realized that perhaps he had underestimated the intelligence of the Red Hand. A criminal bold enough to strike at the Spider probably would have anticipated such an entrance as he now was making, and would have covered this approach also. The watchman who operated the elevator seemed to expect him. Yet his footfalls brought no answer save echoes.

Were they waiting until he had transacted his business with Ransome and prepared to leave? Perhaps, but more probably, no. Behind the watchman, Wentworth unbuttoned his coat, rolled his shoulders to clear his guns for swift action as the elevator mounted swiftly.

Ransome's office, at the end of a long corridor on the twentieth floor, showed the only light. The elevator gate made a tremendous clangor and wind soughed in the shaft as the cage dropped. Wentworth's advance seemed entirely casual, but under his hat's low brim, his eyes kept brilliant watch. No pause at Ransome's door. His pace accelerated and he went through striding, brought up sharply against a railing that cut the office in half.

The rear wall was a steel and ground-glass partition containing a door without a legend. A second door opened in the right hand wall and the furniture, a row of steel filing cabinets, plainly concealed no one. Wentworth saw these things in a glance and his eyes came to a rest on the girl who sat behind the railing. She was coming rigidly to her feet, a dark, angry little thing, neat in a blue knitted suit. Her black eyes studied him openly, her bright mouth drawn into an indignant bow.

"Mr. Ransome is waiting for you," she said shortly.

Wentworth smiled while his ears kept acute watch over the door and hallway behind him.

"Are you sure?" he asked.

The girl shrugged and pivoted on a high heel, pulled open the

RICHARD
WENTWORTH

door in the right hand wall. "The gate's unfastened," she said.
"Mr. Ransome, the man you were expecting is here."

Wentworth knew abruptly that if this was the trap no shooting was scheduled yet. He stepped over the railing instead of using the gate and went swiftly through the door she opened. Inside, he stopped and frowned. The man behind the desk was not the lawyer, Ransome, but a police lieutenant Wentworth knew by sight. Samuelson. Lieutenant Samuelson's lips relaxed in surprise.

"Mr. Wentworth!" he stammered. "But why are you…?" He caught himself and his lips tightened. "Close the door, Miss Morval!" The sharp closing of the door blended with another sound Wentworth could not identify, like the opening of a small window. But it came from behind him. Wentworth was, as always, in danger, poised for action. His taut muscles hurled him sharply to the right, and the hot blast of a bullet fanned his cheek!

Deliberately, ready hands on his guns, Wentworth flung himself toward the floor, turning a shoulder to roll and come up on his feet. He kept his eyes on Lieutenant Samuelson where he stood behind the desk. He saw Samuelson's head wrench upward, his shoulders jerk and the back arch as his whole body gave to a violent blow. Samuelson brought up hard against the wall. For what seemed seconds, the man's rigid muscles held him braced there, eyes horribly popped. Then the stiffening went out of him and he sagged out of sight behind the desk. Where his head had rested against the wall, there was a hideous smear. **ALL THAT** happened in the instant Wentworth took to roll, to come up on his feet and whirl, guns in hand, toward the spot from which the shot had come. The snouts of his twin automatics were trained on a small pass-window between the two offices, but—the window was closed, a blank pane of opaque glass!

Wentworth's forward surge carried him to the door in a long jump. He whipped a gun under his arm to free a hand for the knob, turned a shoulder to ram the door wide. The door was snatched open before him. He slammed full force into the girl who had ushered him in.

Her scream was a gasp. She went down flat on her back, arms and knees jerked up to protect herself. Wentworth stumbled, half-recovered, bounced full force against the metal and glass partition. The glass bellied away, then burst inward across Wentworth's shoulders. A solid sheet drove him to his hands and knees, exploded all around him in glittering shards—

And the outer office door whanged inward. A man without hat or coat sprang to the railing with a stubby revolver in his hand.

"Bubbles!" he cried. "Bubbles, are you hurt? Why, damn you!" The gun jutted toward Wentworth. "Freeze that way, you damned crook, or by God...."

The girl pushed up dizzily, fumbling with one hand at her hiked-up skirt. Her head rolled. "In there," she gasped. "He... he shot..." The whites of her eyes showed, and she sagged back to the floor in a faint.

Both of Wentworth's hands were flat on the floor, one on top of a gun. The other automatic he had dropped in the collision. Impossible to shift his weight off his gun hand and use the weapon before the man could shoot.

"You damned fool," he gasped. "Somebody shot Lieutenant

Samuelson through the pass-window. From the office behind this partition." He jerked his head toward the partition whose glass was shattered. "If we're quick...."

"Keep both hands flat on the floor," the man ordered harshly.

Wentworth stared at him, at the grim long thrust of the jaw, the direct glare of the eyes. The man would shoot, and from the way he held the revolver he would hit his target. But, damn it, the assassin was getting away, the man who had attempted to kill Wentworth... Wentworth's thoughts brought up sharp. No, damn it, the man had not tried to kill him. The gunman had hit his target, Lieutenant Samuelson! The trap was sprung, and Richard Wentworth was fairly caught. A neat frame-up. He....

Wentworth's eyes desperately studied the face of the man with the gun. He was calling anxiously to the girl, trying to rouse her, but there was no wavering in that lined muzzle, no side flicker of the eyes. Abruptly, Wentworth realized that even if he could distract the man's attention, he could not shoot him. Whoever else was involved, he thought, this man was not party to the frame-up. Square, clean faces like that didn't go with crookedness, nor that fine direct eye. Some friend of the girl, here to protect her....

"Listen," Wentworth said quietly. "Listen to me. Put anger out of your mind for a moment. I came here tonight expecting a trap by criminals. When I walked into that other office, somebody opened the pass-window between that office and this and shot Samuelson. The assassin must be in this office now. It doesn't matter whether you believe me or not. I'll back up across the office where you can watch me. For God's sake, look in this space behind the partition, but look carefully...."

The man stared at him, started to shake his head, then said curtly, "All right. But if this is a trick, damn you, I'll...."

Wentworth moved swiftly, backing until his shoulders hit the wall and the man stepped over the railing and moved toward the partition, sidling along so that he could peer through the broken glass. He laughed shortly. "It's empty."

Wentworth's anger sprang up brightly. "You're lying, or else... Wait! Is there a door into another office?"

"There is," the man said shortly, "but I'm through looking. You'll stand right there until the cops come." He edged to the girl's desk and caught up a telephone. "I want a policeman. Damned fast!" he said, into the transmitter.

Wentworth thought swiftly. He might devise an escape when the girl recovered consciousness and distracted the man's attention—she was already stirring—but Samuelson had called him by name, and two persons had seen his undisguised face He must stay and see it through.

"Would you mind," he said, as the man hung up the phone, "calling Commissioner Kirkpatrick now? Tell him Richard Wentworth asks him to come here at once."

"You're *Wentworth!*" the man's eyes widened. "I know you've worked with Commissioner Kirkpatrick on some important cases, but Bubbles said... He said..." He shrugged. "I'll call the Commissioner anyway."

Wentworth heard him identify himself to Kirkpatrick as "Donald Blaine, former detective, second grade, sir."

21

COMMISSIONER KIRKPATRICK was scarcely ten minutes behind the first of the radio police patrol to arrive. He came in striding briskly, a man of Wentworth's height, saturnine of mien and austerely perfect in his dress. Wentworth noticed that, even in his patent haste, he had stopped to pin the inevitable gardenia to the lapel of his dinner coat.

"What's the matter, Dick?" he asked Wentworth in his crisp, authoritative tone.

Wentworth smiled ruefully. "Lieutenant Samuelson was murdered in the next office, and...."

"Samuelson! *Murdered!*" Kirkpatrick's long lips closed in a bitter line. He loved the men of his force with the fierce pride of a commander of loyal troops. Their injuries hit him with a personal and peculiar force. He said slowly, "Go on, Dick."

"With some justice," Wentworth proceeded, "this man and woman think I killed him. The evidence is pretty strong against me, Kirk."

Kirkpatrick grunted, "Nonsense." His eyes swung to the man who called himself Donald Blaine and the girl, Bubbles Morval. She had fully recovered now, though she was still pale. She stepped forward sharply from the protective curve of Blaine's arm.

"Nonsense, your eye!" she said sharply. "He was in there alone with Lieutenant Samuelson. I don't know who he is or why you're trying to protect him, but the minute the door was shut, he shot the lieutenant!"

Kirkpatrick brushed at his spiked mustache with the first knuckle of his right hand, an invariable habit when he was worried, as well he might be. They had fought side by side against many a criminal combination, Wentworth and Kirkpatrick, and they had a deep mutual respect, an affection as strong as close brothers. But Kirkpatrick was a man of stern duty. Friendship would not budge him a hair from the course that his conscience deemed just. Their affection could not have been so close had Kirkpatrick been otherwise.

He nodded jerkily at the girl, went past her into the office where Samuelson lay. He stood for a moment beside the man's body, head bowed. There was a weight on his shoulders, too, as he came back, glancing swiftly about the room. He stopped once and picked up what Wentworth saw was an automatic, undoubtedly the one he had dropped in darting from the office. There was a rasp in Kirkpatrick's voice when he spoke.

"Your story first, Dick."

"Do you mind, Kirk," Wentworth said quietly, "if the others talk first?"

Bubbles Morval was instantly angry again. Her whole small body seemed to vibrate.

"So that you can make your story fit!" she said sharply. "Listen, Mr. Commissioner, if this is going to be a whitewash I'm going to call Mr. Ransome before you start accusing me of killing that officer!"

Kirkpatrick allowed the briefest of smiles to cross his grim lips. "I'm afraid you don't trust the police, young lady."

"Why should I?" Bubbles Morval stood directly in front of Kirkpatrick, her dark head tipped back to glare up into his face. "Didn't you kick out the best cop who ever joined your rotten force? Didn't you fire Don here on a plain frame-up, and ruin his reputation so all he can get to do is bodyguard one of these rich dolls, and…."

Don Blaine touched her on the shoulder. "Don't, honey," he said. "Honest, Commissioner, I never said a thing like that. My trial was fair."

The girl shook off his hand. "I don't care. They should have let you off. They knew that damned Taug was just framing you, and…."

Kirkpatrick was frowning. "I'm sorry about this," he said. "Now wait a minute, Miss… Morval, is it? Yes. Blaine was accused of consorting with criminals. He was sitting at the table with Taug in a nightclub and furnished an alibi for Taug when a gangster rival was shot. He never denied that."

"Why was he there?" the girl cried.

Kirkpatrick brushed his mustache thoughtfully. "As I recall, he said he had been tipped off that there would be a shooting of some sort and he was keeping an eye on Taug. He had made a report to headquarters about it. Taug saw him watching and, as a joke, invited Blaine to share his table." He shrugged slightly. "That it, Blaine?"

"Yes, sir," Blaine said hurriedly. "I never kicked, sir. It was a fool thing for me to do and I deserved what I got. It gave the whole force a black eye. Listen, Bubbles, cut it out! Commissioner Kirkpatrick is okay."

The girl still glared resentfully, but allowed Blaine to pull her away. Kirkpatrick shook his head, "I was always sorry about that,

Blaine. I wanted to reinstate you, but… Well, Dick, your story first then. How was Samuelson… murdered?"

WENTWORTH OPENED his lips to begin with Laskar and then remembered with shocking force that across the airshaft from Laskar's office lay the body of a man branded with the seal of the Spider! God, that had been close! He must lie, then, about his reason for coming to Ransome's office, and he must fool Kirkpatrick, too, about the reason he had begun to speak, then stopped himself. He smiled slightly.

"The Spider once took an interest in Michael Taug, whom Ransome is defending," Wentworth said quietly. "I thought it a good idea to drop in and talk with Ransome. I wanted to warn him that if he resorted to unethical tricks in the defense I would personally see that he was disbarred!"

Kirkpatrick's lips folded grimly against a smile that tugged at his mouth corners. It would not occur to him that Wentworth would lie about so bold a venture, and he had flatly told Wentworth many times that he was convinced Wentworth and the Spider were the same man, though he had never been able to prove that fact. If he ever did, Wentworth knew, their friendship would gain him no slightest consideration… But Kirkpatrick let pass the equivocation about the Spider. Wentworth told then the full details of his stay in Ransome's office, including the curious fact that he had seemed to be expected!

"I had heard from private sources that Ransome would be in his office tonight," Wentworth explained, and described how the shot which had killed Samuelson had seemed to come from the pass-window.

25

Kirkpatrick strode sharply into the space behind the smashed glass partition, examined the door that led into another office.

"The door is locked now," he called. "Search the floor, Sergeant Reams!"

Two men left hurriedly, and Kirkpatrick came back to frown over the automatic pistol he had picked up in the room where Samuelson lay. He kept turning it over in his hand while he heard the stories of the girl and Blaine. Bubbles Morval admitted she had not seen Wentworth shoot. Kirkpatrick nodded and lifted the gun to his nostrils, then jerked startled eyes to Wentworth.

"Didn't you say you hadn't fired a shot?" he demanded.

Wentworth nodded. "Not from any gun in this office," he said flatly.

Kirkpatrick's eyes bore hard on his. "This one has been fired," he said.

Wentworth stared at the gun and felt a cold weight strike at the pit of his stomach. Abruptly, he recognized that automatic, knew it was the one he had missed in Laskar's office. That rubbed place on the butt identified it without question. And he knew suddenly, not only that this gun had been fired as Kirkpatrick had said, but that *Samuelson had been killed by this gun!*

It was damnably clear, and damnably clever. That gun had been stolen from Laskar's office for just this purpose. And he was trapped. By God, the Red Hand planned well!

CHAPTER 3
THE NET TIGHTENS!

WENTWORTH'S BRAIN raced furiously as he sought a way out of the Red Hand's trap. Kirkpatrick was waiting, the look in his eyes suddenly almost pleading. But he must speak, explain....

"Was that gun near the pass-window?" Wentworth asked slowly, to gain time.

Kirkpatrick nodded curtly. That was plain then. The assassin had fired his murder shot through the pass-window, dropped his weapon through—and disappeared. His guess that the death bullet had come from this automatic was confirmed.

Still slowly, Wentworth went on, "I dropped my second gun when I ran into Miss Morval in the doorway there.

Didn't you find another forty-five automatic there?" He hung on Kirkpatrick's reply, but felt that he knew it even before the commissioner spoke.

"Dick," Kirkpatrick's voice was also slow, heavy, "there is no other gun in that office. But a nitrogen test will prove absolutely if you haven't fired a gun within the last few hours." His voice, too, was begging Wentworth, begging him to explain and to do it well!

Fierce laughter rose in Wentworth's throat. The nitrogen test would only draw the net of evidence more tightly about him! For he had fired a gun within the last several hours—at the machine gunner! God! Was there no way out?

He knew what had happened to his own unfired gun, of

Pivoting, Wentworth hurled the
chair, legs first, at Sergeant Reams.

course. He remembered now that there was a second door in the office where Samuelson had died. While he and Blaine had argued, someone had slipped in through that door and picked up the gun that would have proved his innocence. If only he had been able to explain about shooting the machine gunner at Laskar's office! But that chance was more dangerous than the present dilemma. For to admit killing the gunner meant that he confessed he was the Spider!

Kirkpatrick said sharply, "Well, Dick?"

Wentworth braced himself. If he had guessed the Red Hand's frame-up would be so complete....

A man came excitedly into the office, followed by Sergeant Reams, a portly, stubby man whose iron-gray hair bushed out beneath an expensive panama. When he spoke, his voice had a surprising depth and timbre.

"What in the name of all that's holy?" he said slowly. "You, Commissioner. Miss Morval? Ah! So you caught the culprit?"

"What do you mean, Mr. Ransome?" Kirkpatrick asked quietly.

Ransome shrugged, spread his expressive hands, "A man who said he was the Spider phoned me today to assemble all the evidence I had in Taug's favor, to place it in an envelope with ten thousand dollars and have it ready for him at midnight. He said that while Taug might be innocent of the charges against him— which, I may say, he is!—Taug nevertheless deserved prison and the Spider intended him to go there! Naturally, I communicated with the police and Lieutenant Samuelson was good enough to take my place tonight...."

Wentworth's face flushed angrily. "This is a frame-up, Kirkpatrick," he said flatly. "The whole thing from beginning to end is a frame-up. The Spider would never do such a thing as that, and...."

30

"Stop!" Kirkpatrick lifted his head sharply. For a moment his gaze locked with that of Wentworth and when he went on his voice was coldly determined. "Richard Wentworth, I have to warn you that anything you say may be used in evidence against you. I arrest you on a charge of suspicion of murder!"

The group stood transfixed.

Wentworth forced relaxation on his anger-stiffened muscles. Even while he realized that this order might seal his death warrant, he knew a pride in his friend, in the integrity which motivated Kirkpatrick's every action.

"Sergeant Reams, handcuff Wentworth," Kirkpatrick went on, his voice wooden. "I will hold you strictly accountable for his safe delivery to headquarters. He is dangerous and tricky. If he tries to escape—" For an instant, Kirkpatrick's eyes flicked again to Wentworth and there was suffering in their depths. Suffering, but no weakness, no swerving. "If he makes any attempt to escape—*Dick, you hear me!*—then, Sergeant Reams, I order you to… shoot to kill!"

SERGEANT REAMS sprang into brisk action. The handcuffs snapped on Wentworth's wrists and Reams stepped back with his long-barreled revolver in his hand—and he wore a marksman's badge on his breast. Wentworth nodded his compliments to the officer. Now that the blow had actually fallen, he was calmer. He could even smile as the attorney, Ransome, praised the girl—he called her Bubbite Morval, a curious name. French, obviously.

"It was she who really arranged everything," Ransome explained to Kirkpatrick.

The commissioner nodded, bowed stiffly to Bubbite Morval. Wentworth scrutinized both Ransome and the girl. One of them might well be an ally of the Red Hand. It was possible they were merely cat's-paws, but whoever had laid this trap had known precisely the layout of the offices, even to the pass-window, and had obtained keys to the several doors. These things might have been accomplished without inside help, but the assistance of the girl would be invaluable. There was the further fact that the assassin had been hidden in the office just behind where the girl sat; and that, though the collision with him might have been accidental, it had effectually prevented any pursuit! If he could prove that she was an associate and employee of criminals....

"I'll want to communicate with my lawyers," Wentworth said shortly. "Ram Singh is waiting downstairs. I don't suppose you'll mind my giving him a message for Nita? Oh, forget it, Kirk! If you think I'm planning to use him for an escape... I give you my word of honor not to attempt an escape on the way to headquarters. Satisfactory?"

A smile relaxed the grim set of Kirkpatrick's lips. "Perfectly," he said. "Sergeant, you may remove the handcuffs—until we reach headquarters!"

Ransome thrust forward. "Commissioner, I hold you responsible! If this man escapes...."

Kirkpatrick whipped about. "You heard him give his word of honor, I think?" he said harshly. "I am not accountable to you, Ransome, but I will say this. I would rather accept Dick Wentworth's word of honor than to have your oath—or any other man's—supported by a fifty thousand dollar bond. Sergeant?" As Reams holstered his revolver and unfastened the manacles, Kirkpatrick turned back to Wentworth. "I'll want to hear your message to Ram Singh, of course."

Wentworth's words to Ram Singh were brief when he signaled him on the street. "I've been arrested for murder," he told the Sikh. "Tell the *missie sahib* to call my attorneys. Also tell her that I believe Ransome's secretary, Bubbite Morval, is an ally of the Red Hand. And, by the way, Ram Singh, I have given my word to go to headquarters. Understood?"

There was rage in Ram Singh's dark eyes as they flashed to the police. "Understood, *sahib!*" he growled. His *salaam* was elaborate and when he strode away his shoulders were stiff. But he would obey, just as he would have cut Kirkpatrick's throat if Wentworth had signaled for it!

On the way to headquarters, Wentworth refused to discuss further his statement concerning Bubbite Morval. He could see that Kirkpatrick was gravely worried.

"So far as I am personally concerned, Dick," he said. "I do not doubt your word on Samuelson's death. However, on the evidence… I'm afraid you won't find the district attorney so credulous."

Wentworth moved a hand impatiently. This was fruitless. "Were there many reports of crimes tonight before you left?" he asked. "I'm asking particularly about murders."

Kirkpatrick stared at him speculatively before he answered. "There have been no more murders like Laskar's, if that's what you mean," he said slowly.

"Laskar!" Wentworth cried, in simulated surprise. "The Spider's contact man! Has he been killed?"

Kirkpatrick explained, with curt impatience. "And there were two other killings, but not like Laskar's. A watchman was tortured to death by safe robbers, the Bal Masque Theater was robbed of the night's receipts, and a girl usher was killed atrociously. If it had not been for the robbery, you might almost think it the work of some maniac!"

WENTWORTH TRIED to fit that information into what he was beginning to guess about the Red Hand's activities, but had arrived at no conclusion when the car reached police headquarters. He was handcuffed before Sergeant Reams, gun once more in hand, escorted him to Kirkpatrick's barren office on the second floor.

"Young lady waiting to see you, sir," a uniformed man reported to the commissioner. "Miss Clare Sutton. She wants to swear out a warrant, but said she had to talk to you first."

Kirkpatrick frowned, went striding up the stairs ahead of Reams and Wentworth. "Come right in, Sergeant," he called over his shoulder, "and bring the prisoner. My orders still hold good!"

Clare Sutton? Wentworth frowned over the name. In some way, he associated it with Ransome... When he saw the girl, met the heavy-lidded regard of her eyes, he remembered. She was the daughter of Randolph Sutton, formerly Ransome's law partner. She nodded recognition, and her eyes widened at sight of the handcuffs before she turned back to Kirkpatrick. She was a lithely built, graceful girl with hair like tarnished red gold.

"So I want Blaine arrested," she said. "He was supposed to watch over me tonight, my private bodyguard, and he deserted his post and these three men stopped my car and took all my jewels. Blaine is their accomplice! I'm sure of that. He already has a criminal record...."

Kirkpatrick's voice cut in sternly. "Blaine has no criminal record! If I were you, Miss Sutton, I would be careful of making charges without more justification. What you do in the matter of swearing out a warrant is your own concern. Fortunately, Blaine would have ample redress in the courts. If you failed to prove your charge—as I feel confident you would—he could collect to the tune of thousands of dollars for false arrest!"

Clare Sutton laughed. "You rather stand behind your men. Even the men you fire for crookedness, don't you, Commissioner?" she said softly. She turned away casually, moved toward the door.

"Just a minute, Miss Sutton," Kirkpatrick snapped. "Let me ask you a question! Why did you go to the office of Ben Laskar at about six o'clock tonight?"

Wentworth started at the question. Six o'clock! Why, it was a few minutes after six that Laskar had first called his home to try to locate him! Had that been done as a result of this girl's call?

Clare Sutton shrugged one gracefully rounded shoulder. "I was hoping not to be asked about that," she admitted ruefully, "after I read of his death in the papers... Just business, Commissioner. You knew, didn't you, that Laskar was a bookie? I owed him some money on a horse that didn't come home."

Wentworth studied her narrowly as she answered, but could

not decide whether she was lying. Still, there was the coincidence of her call and Laskar's attempt to reach him. Surely, Laskar had not been injured at that time?

Kirkpatrick said drily, "I see. Hold yourself in readiness for questioning, Miss Sutton. Laskar left his office just after you were there and when he came back, he was… *murdered!*"

Once more Clare shrugged. At the door, she murmured, "You've been so helpful, Commissioner."

Wentworth frowned as he noticed that as Clare's shoulder touched the edge of the door, she flinched. He became conscious now that she bore herself very stiffly as if… as if her back were sore. What the devil was the meaning of that? Now that his attention was attracted, he discovered what might be a bruise there on the white flesh of her shoulder, another where her burnished hair had been brushed forward across the temple.

He said softly, "Did these robbers beat you up, Miss Sutton?"

The girl's eyes whipped toward him with a widened stare that might be amazement—or terror! It was only for a moment, then her lids dropped quickly again.

"They did, rather," she said. She left abruptly, and Kirkpatrick's concentrated gaze met Wentworth's.

"What did you mean by that question?" the commissioner demanded shortly. "What do you know about the robbery?"

Wentworth explained, but did not say that he doubted the girl's word, though he did. Robbers might strike a woman they were robbing, but they would not beat her across the shoulders and back. That bore all the marks of a flogging! But her father, old Randolph Sutton, was incapable of that… or was he?

Wentworth had a deep crease between his eyes. What possible connection could Clare Sutton have with the frame-up, with Laskar's death—this daughter of Ransome's former partner? He shook his head, but on one thing his mind was made up. The Spider would pay her a call!

WENTWORTH STROLLED toward Kirkpatrick's desk, hearing Sergeant Reams keep careful pace behind him, "Off hand," Wentworth said, "I should judge that Clare Sutton has fallen in love with her bodyguard and knows that he was with the Morval girl tonight. Sutton is one of those men with a penchant for uplift, isn't he? Hires nothing but ex-convicts and similar employees."

Kirkpatrick jerked his head, "These spoilt daughters of the rich!" He was leafing through a pile of reports laid on his desk during his absence.

"I seem to remember," Wentworth continued softly, "that Clare has shown bizarre taste before this in her boyfriends. Six months ago, she was going everywhere with Michael Taug. Remember? She stopped, all at once."

Kirkpatrick brushed aside talk of the girl with a sharp movement of his hand. His face was pale, deadly grim. "Dick, you'll have to talk and tell me what you've found out about his new criminal! Put aside this subterfuge about Laskar. You were there in his office tonight and you know it! Damn it, man, these reports list six other murders tonight, and every one of them a horror! Two other girls, one of them in the Wakefield Dairy offices, one of them in her own apartment, were killed as that usher was at the theater. Three watchmen and a private police guard. These robberies…."

He fingered the reports "Seven safe robberies. Eight holdups of theaters, parties, nightclubs. And not a single capture. The loot will run into thousands on thousands! And six lives lost! God Almighty, Dick, if you know anything…."

Wentworth stood with set jaw. Slowly, he shook his head. "That's just the trouble, Kirk. I don't know a damned thing more than you do!"

He had intended to make a fight against the murder charge through legal channels to avoid the handicap of police pursuit. But he knew, without doubt now, what he had guessed in that first moment when he had stood beside Laskar's mutilated body: that a new and mighty power was arising in the underworld. Such an outburst of robbery and murder could come from no other source. If the combine were to be smashed, it must be done now before it gathered too much strength. Wait, and dozens of other lives would be sacrificed on the altar of greed. The Spider must strike at once, tonight… He must escape!

During recent months of comparative quiet, he had been building up a new identity in the underworld; had spent days at a time in the haunts of crooks in the guise of a small-time cracksman known as Blinky McQuade. He had a squalid room east of the Bowery. He had intended to use this second personality as a means of ingress to the underworld and its grapevine rumors. Now, it might well prove a sanctuary, a place of refuge for a fugitive and pursued Dick Wentworth! If he could once get free of police surveillance… If? But he *must!*

Wentworth moved quietly to a chair before Kirkpatrick's desk, hearing the measured tread of Sergeant Reams as he moved, so that he would have a clear shot without endangering the commissioner. Sergeant Reams was taking his orders literally. He would shoot without hesitancy. And yet the Spider must escape! Secretly, he surveyed the office he knew so intimately, weighing his chances.

Kirkpatrick's broad desk, its end to the two large windows, was directly opposite the office's only door. This door was flanked by two teletype machines connected with all police precincts. Aside from those, the desk and chairs, there were no furnishings—except a wastepaper basket.

Wentworth teetered back on two legs of the chair, considering that wastepaper basket. It was nearly full.

SEEMINGLY ABSENT-MINDED, Wentworth moved his manacled hands toward his pockets, glanced up in a startled way at Reams' challenge.

"Sorry, Sergeant," he said, smiling, "I want a cigarette."

Kirkpatrick's eyes rested on him suspiciously, but he slid forward a cigarette box and lighter, watched while Wentworth got one going and then leaned back again in the chair. Wentworth puffed rapidly, long inhalations that built a fierce coal at the tip of the cigarette. He rocked gently forward and back on the chair's two rear legs while he watched Reams secretly out of his eye corners. Suddenly, Wentworth appeared to lose his balance and the chair teetered dangerously backward. He threw his hands high.

"Don't try anything!" Reams rasped out.

"Try anything!" Wentworth gasped. "Why, damn it...."

The chair went over backward, slammed to the floor carrying Wentworth with it. Reams crouched forward, gun ready. Kirkpatrick snapped to his feet. Wentworth saw with satisfaction that he had to jerk open his desk drawer to get a gun.

"It's a trick, sir!" Reams cried sharply. "Keep away from him, Commissioner!"

Wentworth staggered to his feet and Kirkpatrick laughed. "That's a hell of a way to try to escape, Dick," he said. "Or were you attempting suicide?"

Wentworth grinned. "Go to hell. Do you think I'd be fool enough to try anything with that sharp-shooter watching me?"

Reams said harshly, "Put that chair down, Mr. Wentworth!"

Wentworth agreed amiably and set the chair where it had been before. "Do you mind if I read a bit of the incoming reports?" He sauntered toward the teletype, beside which stood another chair, but managed a side glance at the wastepaper basket. So far, his stratagem had not been detected. His fall, and the concentration of the two men upon him, had kept them from seeing him snap the fiercely glowing cigarette into the wastepaper. Now he had moved across the room to hold the sergeant's attention. From his eye corners, he watched Reams closely.

Reams watched Wentworth.

It was all of two minutes before Kirkpatrick rasped out a curse that made Reams' eyes flick toward him for a moment.

"The wastepaper basket's on fire!" Kirkpatrick said sharply. "Sergeant...."

Reams swung half about toward the desk and Wentworth

spun into the smooth action that he had planned from the beginning. His hands grasped the chair beside him. Pivoting, he hurled the chair, legs first, straight at Sergeant Reams—and on a level with that deadly gun! Directly in its wake, Wentworth charged across the office. In order to hit him with a bullet, Reams would have to leap aside, and that would take time… Reams lost his head and fired.

The chair smothered the bullet. Before he could shoot again, the chair drove him back against the wall. In the next instant, Wentworth was upon him. Caroming against the wall so that the sergeant's body was between him and Kirkpatrick, he struck out with the handcuffs. He seized the collapsing officer and fell with him to the floor, snatched the revolver from his relaxing hands. For the first time now, he could look toward Kirkpatrick. The commissioner's gun was leveled, but he dared not fire for fear of hitting Reams. With hard-set lips, Kirkpatrick wheeled to circle his desk and get in range. He held his revolver raised, ready to drop on the target. From the hard purpose of his stride, Wentworth knew he could expect no mercy. Then, for a brief moment, Wentworth had his chance. Kirkpatrick was in profile as he strode around the desk, his lifted gun silhouetted against the white wall, a perfect though fleeting mark.

Only such a marksman as the Spider could have done the thing he did then, but Wentworth was more than expert with guns. When he had undertaken his hazardous service, he had known that time after time not only his own survival, but the fate of thousands, would hinge on the accuracy of his weapons—and he spent hours firing at all types of targets from every

conceivable position. He had performed hundreds of more diffi-
cult shots than this one. His bullet smacked the pistol from
Kirkpatrick's hand as though it were a child's toy. And Wentworth sat up, gun still leveled with his two hands.

"Don't make me shoot again, Kirk," he said quietly.

Kirkpatrick stood wringing his numbed gun hand. Alarm
bells were clanging, men shouting in the corridors.

"This way!" Kirkpatrick cried clearly. "If anyone attempts
to leave my office, shoot to kill!" He faced Wentworth quietly
across the width of the office. "It was a good try, Dick, but you
don't stand a chance to escape. Better surrender quietly."

CHAPTER 4
THE RED HAND STRIKES

WENTWORTH MADE no reply to Kirkpatrick's
appeal. He was crouching now astride the unconscious
policeman, holding the gun on Kirkpatrick with his right hand
while his left, moving within the narrow scope of the manacle
chain, groped in the pocket where he had seen Reams place the
handcuff key, quickly found it.

"I want your word not to interfere, Kirk," he said shortly.
"Otherwise, I'll have to knock you out."

Kirkpatrick shook his head. "Dick, you're making a bad
mistake. This will only confirm people in the belief that you
killed Samuelson."

Wentworth nodded agreement. "I know, but it might take
me weeks to prove my innocence, and meantime there's a great

deal of work to be done. This new menace… The Spider might need help, you know!"

He was talking partly to divert Kirkpatrick's attention while he twisted his wrists awkwardly to use the handcuff key. The gun no longer bore directly on Kirkpatrick… Wentworth's right hand came free and he waited for no more. Already men were pounding into the outer office. Wentworth snapped a shot low through the door so that it dug into the floor just beyond.

"Halt! I'll drop the first four men that come through that door!" Wentworth shouted. "Your Commissioner is in my power!"

It was strange that, as Wentworth strode toward Kirkpatrick, the commissioner's eyes were closed; strange that he stood so rigidly with his hands at his sides—or did he think that Wentworth could not strike if he stood, unresisting, like that?

Wentworth caught his breath, set his teeth rigidly. He *had* to escape at once, or… He clenched his fist, stepped in—and Kirkpatrick sprang on him with a shout! His movement only intensified the force of Wentworth's blow. It connected solidly to the jaw and Kirkpatrick went limp, sagged to the floor. Once more, Wentworth threw a bullet through the door.

"Stay back, damn you!" he ordered. "Remember, I drop the first men who enter!"

With two strides then, he reached the broad window and stepped upon the sill. He was thirty feet above the concrete— and there was no way to reach the ground. There was, however, a narrow ledge along which a man with strong nerves could make his way. Wentworth unlocked the manacles from his left wrist, tossed them inside, and without hesitance started upon his perilous path.

Twice, in the short distance he must traverse, his leather soles slipped and he was saved only by the powerful grip of his fingers, but he made the next window. The ceaseless hammer of the alarm bells stood him in good stead. They covered the sound as he opened the window and he was able to slip unobserved into a darkened office—just in time. Police were pouring out into the street, eyes turned upward toward the windows. All exits to the building were undoubtedly closed now, but for a few minutes the windows on the opposite side of the building would not be watched. If only he had with him that fine silken rope which men called the Spider's web! Abruptly Wentworth uttered a soft laugh. He had no rope, but at a half dozen places in the building there were fire hoses!

A few moments later, he had slipped across a momentarily empty hall and was unreeling a fire hose, securely coupled to a water outlet, out of a window to the ground. It made a splendid rope. He slid down it to the street, head thrown back. He had almost reached the ground, when a gun spoke above him. A bullet whined close, but he gave them no time for a second shot. He landed lightly, rounded the corner, looked desperately for a taxi. None in sight. Already the empty streets reverberated with the sounds of pursuit, and presently guns began to blast again. He was too far ahead for accurate shooting and the shadows made him a tricky target, but unless he found a taxi quickly, police cars would run him down.

FOR THREE blocks he sprinted, doubling corners, before

he found a cab. He was panting heavily, but his gun took the place of his
voice. The driver of the taxi fled, and
Wentworth flung himself behind the
wheel. Before he had reached the first
corner, he heard the sirens of converg-
ing radio prowl cars. Wentworth's mouth was drawn to a harsh
line. If he could gain five minutes' headway over the pursuit....

He reached awkwardly into the tonneau and switched on the
radio, listened to the even voice of the police announcer weave
a net of radio cars around him. Already orders had been given
to block three main downtown avenues with trucks. The theft
of the cab and its plate numbers had been reported.

"A yellow taxi driven by a man in evening dress. Tail coat.
No hat...."

Only one thing to do and Wentworth acted swiftly. In a dark
side street, he abandoned the cab, doubled back to a subway
entrance. He stopped at the change booth to give the agent
ample chance to identify him, then went up the station beyond
his range of vision. This was the platform at which only trains
bound uptown would stop. Wentworth dropped to the roadbed
and crossed the tracks, vaulted to the downtown platform—still
out of sight of agents on either side. A few moments later, he was
speeding downtown again. At the third station, he alighted and
hailed a cab from a waiting rank. Everything now depended on
speed. Wentworth leaned forward to urge the driver to greater
haste and, abruptly, his body stiffened, his eyes hardened. The cab
was a half block from a motion picture theater whose brilliantly

lighted marquee advertised a midnight performance. And those lights shone on horror!

Beneath the marquee, a man groveled on the pavement, screaming with agony. For a moment his face writhed toward the cab and Wentworth cursed harshly. Where the man's face had been was… the brand of the Red Hand! But damn it, he could not stop now! True, minions of the Red Hand might still be nearby, but police would be here within a few moments. The police who already had been given his description and been told to capture him, dead or alive. He would be too conspicuous in this neighborhood, hatless and in full evening dress. Within twenty minutes, Blinky McQuade could safely return.

"Drive on," Wentworth ordered the taxi man. "And step on it!" The cab was passing the theater when the Red Hand struck again. There was a dull explosion and a sheet of flame swept across the lobby of the house! Instantly, the building itself was afire in a dozen places. Black smoke and yellow tongues of flame flapped and puffed through the foyer.

"Stop!" Wentworth called out to the driver. "Send in a fire alarm. I'll see what I can do here."

He jumped from the braking cab, turned and darted toward the inferno of the theater. Wentworth might flee to avoid danger to himself so as to accomplish, in the end, the greater good for the people he always served. But when the people themselves were menaced, the consideration of his own life and liberty must wait! Already from within, above the dull deep roaring of the flames, he could hear the panic-stricken screams of the trapped audience!

A dark alley ran beside the theater. There would be fire exits there, if the fear-maddened people within could be led that way. Wentworth's face was white as he raced toward them. He knew what panic could do to a crowd! They would fight one another, trample one another to death in a mad milling that accomplished nothing, until the fire claimed them all, unless....

HE REACHED the first of the double fire exits, locked from without. A single push from within should serve to open them, but he could hear fists battering futilely inside, hear screams. God, were these doors *locked?*

Wentworth threw a desperate glance about. Nothing here that might smash them down. His gun... He whipped the revolver from his belt. Only three shots, but if they were properly placed they might smash loose the fastenings. With a frantic calm, Wentworth turned the beam of a small pocket flashlight along the edges of the doors. He cursed savagely. Wholesale murder had been planned here! Small metal wedges had been driven in at top and bottom. There were five of them, but if he could shoot out three....

Almost as the thought glanced across his brain, he pressed the muzzle near the first of the wedges and squeezed the trigger. A shout of triumph burst from him as the powerful blow of the lead wrenched the wedge nearly free. Swiftly, he repeated the action and, with the echo of the last shot, one of the doors exploded outward under the pressure of the panic within. Wentworth was hurled across the narrow alley, driven breathless against the opposite wall. He lashed out, grim-mouthed, at the men who led that rush. Three, four times he struck.

"Quiet!" he shouted. "There is plenty of time for all of you! Take it easy! Stop the rush! The other doors are being opened."

Against that tide of maddened humans, he beat his way forward, knocking down those that fought.

Over the heads of the stampeding mob, he caught sight of a small, quiet group, three women being ushered out by a man who held them out of that frantic rush.

"Inside there, get a fire axe!" he yelled. "You with three women. A fire axe!"

The man's white face lifted to his as he struggled to establish order in that narrow passageway which might so easily become choked with these human sheep. A child was thrown through the opening as if expelled from a gun and Wentworth's arm reached out, his revolver slashed for the skull of a man who was striking about him with his fists. Some semblance of quiet was beginning to settle here at the doorway, but those behind kept up a piercing outcry that bred madness. Already flames ate toward the draft of this opening. Thick smoke swirled and momentarily obscured the interior, drove suffocatingly into Wentworth's face. Despair gripped him. This single narrow opening was not enough and he was powerless to effect more— unless he could get hold of a fire axe.

Wentworth was burning with rage. In God's name, what did the Red Hand hope to accomplish by such carnage as this?

He did not even need that mutilated body beneath the marquee to identify the hand of this new underworld power. That fire had been plainly incendiary, touched off gasoline, or naphtha. And the intention to trap these people was obvious, too, in these wedged fire doors. Deliberately, the Red Hand had sought to slaughter these innocents!

The fire pall lifted for a moment and he glimpsed the man to whom he had cried. He had two fire axes in his hand and was struggling to reach the door. Wentworth plunged to meet him, but the body of the unconscious child in his arm hampered him cruelly. He tried to thrust the child into the arms of a man already wriggling free of the press and the man only struck out wildly.

He would have to carry this child out of danger, then return. Seconds were precious. He looked down at the white, lolling face, his mouth a tortured slit. A hand clutched at his arm and he turned. The woman beside him was middle-aged. Her white hair streamed about her shoulders and one arm hung twisted and limp at her side. Her clothing was torn almost from her body.

"I'll take her," she whispered. "Give her to me."

Wentworth's harsh laughter tore his throat. He and an aged woman against these mad beasts… Tenderly, he gave the child into the woman's one good arm and she staggered away, battered by escaping people, almost knocked off her feet again and again, risking death to save this one small life….

THE SIGHT lent fury to Wentworth's strength and he fought savagely to reach the man with the fire axes. So fierce was his mien that for a space of seconds, even those panic-stricken fools gave way before Wentworth's onslaught. For a space of seconds—but it was enough. Wentworth stumbled through into the flame-choked inferno within. The next instant, the door was choked, jammed again. It took seconds for a single person to wriggle through that mass. Then Wentworth's hand closed on a fire axe. He sprang at the wedged door....

The minutes that followed were a blind and flame-slashed nightmare. Wentworth whirled the axe in crashing blows against stubborn steel and wood, driving doors outward against the wedges. One after another, he forced openings which the Red Hand had intended to yield only to flame and death. His lungs were tortured with the hot knives of fumes and smoke-fouled air. But there could be no pause, no rest....

Wentworth could not tell how he knew finally that his work was finished. He found himself beside a battered door and there was no further press of panic about him, no more screams. Only the deepening roar, the crackling triumph of the flames. He stared about him and the lurid light danced fitfully over an emptied auditorium, empty save for a few who would never stir again.

Wearily, Wentworth dragged himself to that final labor, carrying out the crumpled bodies. Then he saw the black-gleaming slickers of fire department men, felt a hand slap his shoulder and heard a man's hoarse shout.

"Good work, fellow!" the man shouted. "We'll take care of the rest!"

Bone weary, but driven by the fury that still rode him savagely, Wentworth staggered out into the grateful coolness of the night. He coughed stranglingly, wove an uncertain path along the exit alley. Outside, police lines were holding back the curious crowd that had sprung up out of the night. Fire lines were everywhere, the red trucks gleaming in the leaping light of the flames. Well, the Spider's work was done here. He must hurry on now, lest some policeman's keen eye....

A fireman threw an arm about his shoulders. "You need medication, man," he said. "That's smoke poisoning...."

Lest he attract attention, Wentworth went where he was thrust toward an ambulance. There was a line of others awaiting treatment, and Wentworth eased away from it.

Abruptly, a man's voice ripped through the night: "Grab that man! He's wanted for murder!"

With a curse, Wentworth darted off into the night. He recognized that voice. Sergeant Reams! It meant Kirkpatrick was somewhere near, too, for the sergeant went always with the commissioner. Sobbing for breath, Wentworth pelted along the sidewalks, leaped the fire lines before the police on watch there could catch the meaning of that shout. Behind him, the cry rose again:

"Stop that man! He's wanted for murder!"

Frantically, his eyes whipped the street ahead. A rank of cabs stood at the corner, their drivers gone to watch the fire. Yes, that was his chance. His only chance. From somewhere within his mighty heart, he drained the strength to reach those cabs, to wrench one of them away from the curb and start it roaring through the night.

His lips were twisted in a bitter smile. It was this way, always. The Spider fought to save his people, and the police dogged his trail with blazing guns. He rolled his shoulders wearily, concentrated on the task of escaping the pursuit. But they were not to blame, and he did not complain. It was his way. They were the law and his justice took no account of the law they were sworn to uphold.

The thin rising shriek of the sirens burst out behind him. A few blocks now, only a few. If he could hold his lead....

THE POLICE were only three blocks behind when finally he slewed the cab to a halt in the middle of the street and once more fled afoot. When he whirled into Pallin Place, his lead had shortened to fifty feet... He dived to the shelter of a cellar stairway just as the first of the police cars dry-skidded around the corner.

If he could dodge through this tenement without detection, he could reach the court which backed the houses on Pallin Place—and Holian Alley! Once he reached Blinky McQuade's room, he could within minutes destroy the last traces of Richard Wentworth. The cops, if they reached that far, would find only an almost blind small-time crook, shivering with fright under their questions. If he could get to that room! He twisted the knob of the cellar door. It was locked.

He heard other cars whine into the street and stop, heard men shouting to each other.

"He's in this block somewhere!" a hoarse voice called. "In one of these houses. Call headquarters. There are enough of us to hold him in this one block..." Heavy footsteps slapped along the street. "Search those cellar stairways!"

Wentworth's lips grinned back from his teeth. *If he could reach Blinky McQuade's room!* But he first must get through this door. And now the police knew he was in this block, even Blinky McQuade would not be surely safe. They would search every room. If they caught him now, he would be loaded with chains, slammed into a cell. The Red Hand, who could coldly plan such a slaughter as that fire-trap theater, would rage unchecked!

The shouts of the police were drawing nearer.

"Remember!" one of them yelled. "This guy killed Samuel-son!"

Crazy laughter gasped from Wentworth's lips as he fought the unyielding door. He knew what those shouted words meant. The police did not often bother to capture police murder suspects… *alive!*

CHAPTER 5
KILL THE SPIDER!

WENTWORTH FORCED himself to calmness and edged upward on the steep cellar steps until he could see the approaching officers.

Three men were searching across the street. On this side, two were working, the nearest only three buildings away. Wentworth's lips curved in a slight, hard smile. When the nearest policeman was only a half dozen yards away, to Wentworth's left, Wentworth whipped out his fountain pen. He tossed it to his right, into the next dark areaway. The sound, slight as it was, easily reached the ears of the alert officer.

"I think I heard him!" he shouted. He ran swiftly forward, eyes fixed on the stairwell where the pen had landed. As he passed, within a scant yard of where Wentworth lay, Wentworth launched himself from his hiding place in a swift dive.

His hands seized the man's ankles, jerked his feet off the ground. As the officer plunged downward, Wentworth wrenched the gun free, dived back into the stairwell. The entire maneuver had taken only the briefest part of a second. To other police, it seemed only that their companion had fallen....

The cop was shouting now, cursing incoherently. Wentworth flung lead out of his dark pit, shooting high over the man's head, then he turned to the door. Two bullets smashed the lock to bits and he hurled himself forward through the tenement basement at a dead run; up again into the back court and he was sprinting for the rear entrance to No. 1 Holian Alley.

Within two minutes of his attack on the policeman, Wentworth was stripping off his evening dress in Blinky McQuade's room. He bundled it up, flung himself on his knees on the bed. His fingers touched secret springs and opened a panel in the apparently solid, wooden headboard, revealed a brightly lighted mirror, and a door that became a shelf bearing a hundred articles of make-up. Never had Wentworth's skilled fingers moved more rapidly, thrusting into his mouth a prepared pad that made his lower lip pendulous and lax, painting his cheeks with the lotion that made the skin sallow and taut across the cheekbones, penciling in the shadow lines of age. A few moments then to streak his hair with gray and rumple it; to don the ragged clothes of Blinky McQuade....

Already the police were shouting in the court. Their heavy feet were pounding through the hallways of No. 1 Holian Alley. Now they were on this floor... Thirty seconds after he had closed that secret panel and flung himself down on Blinky McQuade's dingy bed, the police were hammering at the door. A sleepy, slattern man whose weak eyes blinked and strained in the light until he got on his thick, hooded glasses, let the officers in. Cringingly, he answered their questions and, presently, the police left.

No man would have mistaken Blinky McQuade, shambling, round-shouldered hanger-on of the underworld, for Richard Wentworth. Gone was the arrogance of carriage, the sturdy confidence of manner. In their place was a grizzle-haired crook who moved always with a certain furtiveness of manner, whose eyes seemed weak behind the thick, hooded spectacles. No one would guess that one lens actually could be focused like a telescope at ranges up to thirty feet! For Blinky McQuade's eyes were supposed to have been injured in a back-flare when he had blown a safe. Since then, he had learned to use his fingers instead of nitroglycerin to tap strongboxes.

It was an hour later that Blinky McQuade left his rooming house and was passed through the police lines by those who had already questioned him. Swiftly, he made his way through the darkened streets. He had promised Nita van Sloan he would phone her at the first opportunity. If she had heard the police radio broadcasts, she would be deeply alarmed. From a dial phone from which a call could not be traced, he called his home. It was Ram Singh who answered and when Wentworth left the booth he was frowning.

Nita van Sloan had eluded the men Wentworth had asked to guard her, had gone about the Spider's business. She had left a note saying that she would keep Bubbite Morval under surveillance. Brave Nita, plunging fearlessly into the work of helping him. God grant that she was safe, for the Spider must press his battle swiftly.

Many a rendezvous of criminals was tucked away in slattern buildings here; probably the most notorious was Balmy's Bit House. It had taken Blinky McQuade weeks to gain an entree, for only the criminally elite were admitted. Perhaps there he could find some news of the Red Hand!

So Wentworth hoped, but when he had crept through the dark alley and up tenement stairs to the very door of Balmy's Bit House, he found himself barred! A steel panel clicked shut behind him and made him prisoner, and through a narrow peephole, Balmy curtly demanded his "card."

"What'de hell are you talking about?" Wentworth made his voice coarse and hard. "What kind of card? This ain't no speakeasy, is it?"

Balmy only grunted. "Shove off, Blinky," he ordered. "My place ain't open no longer to any of you punks who don't have a card!"

He closed the peephole with finality, and behind Wentworth the steel panel slid open, leaving the way to the street free. Wentworth's eyes were narrow and hard behind the thick lenses of Blinky McQuade's glasses. No need to ask what had happened here!

The Red Hand had closed the doors to minor crooks. Well,

there were other places where he might pick up grapevine news of this new ruler of the underworld!

A half dozen blocks from Balmy's, Wentworth ducked down into a basement Chinese laundry, ignored the two Cantonese laboring over ironing boards, and pushed through a curtain at the right side of the store. He was in a dim hallway, then on steps that led downward. At their bottom, a fly-specked electric bulb burned. Wentworth stood under it and spoke into the darkness.

"It's Blinky McQuade for China Sam's."

There were little furtive sounds, then a hulking, broad-shouldered figure slippered into the dim pool of light. Hands folded into broad sleeves, China Sam bowed impassively.

"You got ticket?"

Blinky McQuade shook his fists in the air. "No, I got no ticket! What the hell is all this stuff, a lockout? It's like some damned labor union. No got ticket, no get in!"

China Sam's pockmarked Eurasian face remained still. He bowed again. "No got ticket, no can come in," he said.

"What kind of ticket?" Wentworth asked plaintively.

China Sam slipped off into the dark.

Wentworth cursed harshly before he went up the stairs with the labored tread of Blinky McQuade. What went on behind these guarded doors? What was this "ticket" China Sam and Balmy demanded—a badge from the Red Hand? He felt his face drain as he realized what the fact would mean. It meant… that already the Red Hand ruled the hell that was called the underworld! By God, if Blinky could not enter, the Spider could— and would!

Wentworth's automatic jerked into line and he squeezed the trigger.

Fatigue was working on Wentworth's powerful frame now, and it had been hours since he had eaten. He bought the late edition of the morning papers and slid into an all-night restaurant. While he ate, he scanned the columns with swift efficiency. The story of his escape from headquarters was subordinated to the headlines that shrieked of the theater fire in which nineteen persons had lost their lives and two score others had been badly injured. Nineteen dead! Wentworth's lips closed thinly at the news, but what he was seeking was the reason for this horror....

Ah, the Bank of Trust! That was clear then. First the fire in the theater which had sucked in the police reserves of the whole district, paralyzed the radio patrols. Then, while the cops labored over the rescue, while they had pursued Wentworth through the streets, the criminals of the Red Hand had looted the bank of half a million dollars! The three watchmen had been murdered, as Laskar had been, by the Red Hand! One of them had lived long enough to gasp out that each of the bandits wore in his right hand a mailed gauntlet, blood-red!

Savagely, Wentworth thrust his half-completed food away from him. He must strike now! There were police still on guard in Holian Alley and Pallin Place, watching lest Wentworth escape. But they had already identified and questioned Blinky McQuade.

HE PASSED without hindrance, slipped through the dim-lit halls to the sleazy second floor room of Blinky McQuade. Carefully, he drew down the cracked shade, and opened again the secret panel in the head of the curiously massive bed. Swiftly, he set to work. He plucked out the pad that made his mouth sag and with a few deft touches painted out the lips entirely. Shaggy brows went over his own, a lanky black wig covered the graying hair of Blinky McQuade—and it was the face of the Spider which glared back, glittering-eyed, from the mirror!

From a similar panel compartment in the foot of the bed, Wentworth drew out a black crushable hat, a long black cape which he swiftly made into a bundle. He donned again the conspicuous glasses of Blinky McQuade. It was risky thus for Blinky to pass the police again, and if they should search the bundle, find the habiliments of the Spider! But it was the lesser danger. Any stranger would be stopped. To wriggle through the police cordon in the garb of the Spider would be fatal. Always, the Spider must move furtively. His caped, hunched silhouette was too well known to police and criminals—and too well-hated! At the first glimpse of him, their hungry guns would roar. Yet it must be the Spider who worked tonight. It would take a mighty fear to loosen criminal tongues about this Red Hand which had unionized the underworld, which killed so terribly. And talk they must. The Spider had sworn it!

A block from Balmy's Bit House, Blinky McQuade entered a tenement house. It was the Spider who emerged upon its roof. Swiftly, a hunched sinister silhouette against the night sky, he stole to the building in which Balmy had his place. McQuade had learned of the exit through a trapdoor into a first floor storeroom where piled up boxes made steps. He had found Balmy's private exit, through a closet in his office whose back moved on a central pivot—and opened into a similar closet in the railroad flat next door. But there was a third, simpler way—the fire escape!

Silently as the creature whose name he bore, the Spider crept down the steel steps to Balmy's window. This one on the fire escape would be guarded, but there was another which could be reached by stepping out over space. Standing outside the guard rail, Wentworth got his toe on the sill, closed his gloved fingers on the frame and slowly drew himself across until he could peer into a private room of the Bit House. A grim smile twisted the Spider's mouth. Except for a girl, this room was empty. And the girl was... Bubbite Morval!

Although her back was toward him, he could not be mistaken in the alert challenging poise of her body, her quick movements. No need to look farther. Bubbite should tell the Spider what he wished to know! For an instant he was worried. Nita had planned to follow this girl! Had she walked into Balmy's trap? He shook his head. She would merely have been turned away as he had. Carefully, he got both feet on the sill, crouched to throw up the window and leap through—and the girl twisted about in her chair and her fear-stretched eyes gazed straight into his!

For a space of seconds, she remained rigid, her mouth gaping to scream. Wentworth flung up the casement, ducked in while his gun spun into his hand—and still the girl did not cry out. He reached her in a stride, towered over her where she sat beside a round wooden table.

"Don't make a sound!" he ordered.

Bubbite Morval swallowed noisily and her lips closed, while

fear still glistened in her eyes. When her voice came out, it was clear and challenging.

"Certainly not," she said shortly. "If I'd intended to scream, do you think I'd have waited until you got inside? You don't think I'm afraid of you, do you, Spider?"

Wentworth's smile did ugly things to the make-up distorted mouth of the Spider. "People usually are," he said quietly. "Especially people who ally themselves with criminals—as you have, Bubbles!"

The girl's darkly pert face was pale as she came to her feet. "I don't blame you for thinking that," she whispered, "but there's a difference between what you say, and… Spider, tell me something on your word of honor. Did you ask Ransome for the evidence in favor of Taug?"

Wentworth said, "On my word of honor, Bubbles, no. Why?" He was studying the girl's face keenly, listening, too, for any sign that his entrance had been detected. So far, he heard nothing.

Bubbles Morval cried, "I believe you! Did you know that Richard Wentworth is in jail accused of murder? He's a friend of yours, isn't he? I thought he was guilty, but since you've told me this I'm not so sure."

Was the girl just talking to hold him until help could come? Or was she genuinely trying to be helpful? He said softly, "All right, but you haven't explained why you're here in a criminal hide-out."

Bubbles reached out a hand toward his arm, stopped at the forbidding flash of the Spider's eyes. "I'll tell you," she whispered.

"I haven't long. They'll be coming back in here. But… Did you ever hear of a crook called the Red Hand? He…."

"Drop that gun, Spider!" The man's voice, from the doorway, did not surprise Wentworth. He had been keeping acute watch with ears and eyes. Before the man's last word had been uttered, Wentworth's automatic was in line and he squeezed the trigger. He had just a glimpse of the man before his lead hammered him backward through the doorway, then he had thrown a pinioning arm around the girl.

"If you fight," he said harshly, "I'll have to knock you out! Understand that!"

In a long leap, he had reached the door carrying the submissive girl with him. For a moment, he paused beside the body of the man his bullet had killed, and when he raced on along the corridor where shouts were beginning to rise to bedlam with the echoes of his shot, a crimson spot glimmered on the forehead of the dead man; a seal that would cry to all those who rushed to investigate that shot that the Spider had been here and made his kill!

Before the first men stampeded along that corridor, Wentworth had reached the door of another private room, yanked it open and leaped inside. His gun quested ahead of him, but the room was empty. He put the girl's shoulders to the wall behind the door.

"We have about sixty seconds before they begin to search these rooms," he said. "Perhaps a little more, since the open window will mislead them. Now, will you talk, Bubbles? If you'll tell me all you know about the Red Hand, I'll protect you—

otherwise, I might let it be known via the grapevine that Bubbite Morval told the Spider certain things! I don't imagine the Red Hand would like that, do you?"

The girl shook her head. "Don't kid yourself, Spider. That doesn't frighten me. Why? Because I don't know anything. When I got home tonight, there was a note there signed by the Red Hand. It said that if I came here, I'd be given evidence to clear the name of my fiancé, Don Blaine, who got fired off the police force on a frame-up."

For a moment, Wentworth stared fixedly at the girl, but her eyes met his unwaveringly and he smothered a curse. Perhaps he had been mistaken in her; but that did not help him in his search. He listened intently at the door. Men's feet were trooping past now and, abruptly, one man cried out in a hoarsely terrified voice.

"Look! Look at his forehead. God! The Spider! *The Spider!*"

FOR A moment, there was utter silence in the hallway, then more men's voices burst out crazily and there was a stampede of trampling feet back along the corridor toward the main room of Balmy's Bit House. Wentworth's eyes narrowed. Probably that meant there were nothing but small-time crooks here tonight. Real killers such as the Red Hand used would not flee from the mere presence of a dead man with the Spider's seal on his forehead. Wentworth turned back to the girl.

"All right," he said briefly, "I'm believing you for the present. Run down that hall screaming. Tell them I'm in this room! Hurry!"

Bubbite started toward the door. "Why are you doing this?" she asked hesitantly. "To protect me?"

Wentworth laughed at her. "Do you think I'd waste time on a crook like you to help my plans along?"

The girl's head snapped up. She darted out into the hallway and Wentworth heard her screams rise. He reached up and unscrewed the ceiling light, blew the fuses with a touch of his gun barrel in the socket, then he slipped to the door. Bubbles' screams had receded into a jumbled mutter. The entire place was in darkness. Gun ready in his hand, Wentworth walked soft-footed in the direction the girl had fled. Twenty feet farther along, he opened another door. Just as he ducked from sight, a brilliant flashlight licked down the hallway and he heard men begin a slow-footed advance.

Behind them, he could hear the cracked voice of Balmy. "The chief says it's worth twenty grand to him to have the Spider killed," Balmy was whispering. "Twenty grand to the guy that drills the Spider! Rush him, boys!"

So Balmy had called the Red Hand and got his orders! That was quick work. It was Balmy, then, that the Spider wanted!

He had chosen this room carefully. Through this floor was cut the trapdoor which gave onto the storeroom below. Balmy was a big man. He would be hard to handle, but the Spider thought grimly that he could manage! He waited, and men filed past, soft-footed, clutching guns and flashlights, working toward the door behind which Bubbite Morval had told them he crouched. Balmy's voice still urged them on hoarsely, but Balmy himself drew no nearer. He was keeping well in the background.

NITA VAN SLOAN

Impatiently, Wentworth reshaped his plans. He whipped off cape and wig, tucked them under his vest and, gun in hand, slipped out into the crowd of men in the hallway. Imperceptibly, he slowed his pace, then whispered to the man next to him:

"Why in the hell don't Balmy do his bit, too?"

"Damned right," the man muttered back. "Hiding out back there while we get the Spider!"

Wentworth swore. "I'm going back and get Balmy," he said.

He repeated that again and again while he wove against the seemingly endless stream of gunmen pouring toward the spot where the Spider was thought to be trapped.

"Give up, Spider!" a man was yelling. "You can't get away!"

Wentworth had reached the main room now. "Where's Balmy?" he whispered.

"I'm Sharps," a man said at his elbow. "What d'you want?"

"Balmy," Wentworth told him shortly.

The man gripped his arm. "Balmy's gone to get help," he said. A curse welled against Wentworth's teeth, but he choked it down. Gone to help! Then Balmy would be beyond his reach. Balmy was gone... but Sharps was Balmy's second in charge.

"Quiet," Wentworth said hissingly, "We're going to Balmy's office for a little chat."

"What the hell is this?" Sharps gasped.

"This," Wentworth jabbed harder with the automatic. *"This is the Spider's gun!"*

CHAPTER 6
UNDER THE RED HAND

THE ROOM in which Nita lay was pitch-black. She was bound hand and foot, gagged. She was wretched. She had thrown herself into the Spider's work, followed Bubbles Morval and been ignominiously trapped by Balmy's steel panel. And now she was doomed to face the Red Hand! Heaven help her if he penetrated her disguise as an underworld moll! Yes, Nita, a prisoner in Balmy's was very near despair when she heard the shot and the shout of terror that greeted the finder of the Spider's kill—and hope leaped high in her breast. Somehow, Dick had found where she was and had come to save her!

She strained her ears, listening to the vengeful cries of the gunmen and something of fear for Dick tinged her hopes. But he had not struck blindly. If he had entered this deathtrap, he had a way out.

Nita held her breath, trying to hear through the turmoil, through the pounding of her own pulses. She could not cry out, but she could thump on the floor with her feet, make muffled sounds through the gag.

As the minutes dragged on with no new crescendo of sound, with no more secret footsteps in the dark, Nita began to know the blackness of despair. Her eyes stung with tears... When the door whipped open and light streaked into the room, she turned joyfully. Men with guns in their hands, aching to kill. But the Spider was not here! Nita was jerked roughly to her feet, half-dragged, half-carried out into the hall, the gag torn from her lips. Eagerly her eyes quested for some signs of the man she loved. They rested instead upon... horror!

THE MAN WHO RULED IN HELL

The man stood in the shadowed corner of the big main room. She made out with difficulty that he wore ordinary clothing except that his shirt, like the rest of his garb, was dead black. But that she saw only afterward. What held her terror-widened gaze was the man's face—and his right hand. The eyes and the forehead were the face of a man, but there the likeness stopped, for across his countenance lay the brand of a huge hand, and where that hand had touched—*there was no flesh at all!*

The teeth, wholly exposed, glistened whitely in the somber light, and all the bony structure of nose and cheeks lay hideously bare. It was a mask. It had to be a mask! But she knew what it meant, knew who this man was. His face was a caricature of the faces of those the Red Hand slew and the man's right fist—It *was* the Red Hand! Clad in a steel gauntlet that caught facets of light as he moved it, that fist was a horror, too. For the mailed fingers were stained, horribly stained... Nita felt her head whirl, saw the lights dim before her eyes. But this was very foolish. If it were Dick the Red Hand had tortured... She had to say something, do something. Just in time she remembered her disguise.

"Geez," she gasped, her voice a hoarse travesty, "ain't you the pretty boy! Who in the hell are you trying to scare?"

The Red Hand stretched out that awful mailed fist, and slowly closed the fingers. He said nothing, but the powerful tension, the knowledge of the things that fist had done, were more dreadful than any threat. But she was not supposed to know what that fist could do, Nita told herself. She turned her head away with a shudder.

"Geez, is that guy nuts?" she whispered hoarsely. Her eyes

69

caught sight of Bubbles Morval, pale-faced between two men who gripped her arms. What in God's name did this beast intend to do with them?

When Balmy's voice broke out then, hoarsely from the terrifying shadows, Nita almost screamed. "Hey, Red Hand!" he yelled. " 'Scuse me—I mean Your Majesty— the door to my office is locked and I think I can hear voices in there! We looked every- where else and the Spider ain't nowhere. I can't find Sharps either. Maybe… well, maybe they are off in—"

Before he could finish his sentence, the gaunt mask of the Red Hand was striding through the crowd. Men scattered out of his path in white-faced terror. One did not move rapidly enough. The back of that mailed hand caught him across the face and hurled him senseless against the wall! The men beside her were whispering, "Geez, did you see him lay out Whitey? I want to see him and the Spider get together. You hear what Balmy said? His office. There ain't but one door to that office and no windows. If the Spider's still in there…."

The men thrust Nita toward the hallway where already the hammering of the Red Hand beat hollowly against the walls.

"Open up, Spider!" came a deep, harsh voice. "You can't get out!"

Silence fell over the place, silence while they waited for the Spider's answer. It came instantly, mocking, triumphant—a flat, hollow sound that seemed to beat at them from the walls, that filled the long, dim hallway with its jam of killers and jeered at them—the laughter of the Spider!

For seconds after it had ceased, the silence held, then a roar of anger went up. A gun blasted three times. Men's shoulders thundered against the barred door. Four, five, six times, their weight beat against that barrier before it ripped its hinges and spilled them in Balmy's windowless office. Nita strained upward on tiptoes. A man clambered up on a chair.

"He ain't in there," he said, his voice hushed. "He ain't in there! The Spider… Hell, he just vanished into thin air!"

The relief left Nita limp. A helpless prisoner in the hands of this masked monster, she nevertheless smiled. Dick had found a way out!

AND NOW Nita found herself, with Bubbles Morval and the hard-faced man who had disarmed her at the door—Sharps was his name—all riding together in a closed car. One man in front kept the muzzle of a machine gun trained on the prisoners.

Finally the car stopped in an enclosed area where the muffled engine made a deep-throated sound; the doors were whipped open. Two men jerked Sharps out. In the opening, waiting, stood the Red Hand.

His harsh voice held a mockingly polite note: "If you please, ladies, I have an exhibition for you."

The sound of his voice plucked at Nita's nerves like a knife point, but she kept her mind on Bubbles Morval instead of that Red Hand. She could not understand why Bubbles was a prisoner.

At his gesture two men seized
Sharps and dragged him forward.

"We held an inquiry," the Red Hand was saying as Nita's long-cramped limbs carried her with difficulty from the car. "At first, I was inclined to blame one of you ladies. But I have decided you are innocent. I think you are very lucky."

Nita kept her eyes resolutely away from the man in the ghastly mask. She could hear Bubbles Morval draw in a long,

73

shuddering breath. Her questing eyes revealed that they were in a high-ceilinged basement. She concentrated on the voice of the Red Hand. If she could identify the voice tone—but the mask muffled it, of course.

"Yes," the Red Hand was saying, "the inquiry is over. There was a secret doorway out of Balmy's office which the Spider used. It is quite obvious that Sharps must have revealed it to him...."

"No, no!" Sharps screamed. "I swear I didn't! He already knew it! He just walked into that closet and...."

"You talk too much, Sharps!" The Red Hand interrupted lightly. "Even now when you have been warned, you talk too much. I'm afraid I'll have to... *close your mouth!*"

Sharps screamed. He ran wildly across the basement and brought up blindly against the wall. He bounced away from it, wheeled in a looping circle and started off at another tangent. The Red Hand let him run until he sank sobbing to the ground, then, at his gesture two men seized Sharps and dragged him forward. Nita felt nausea like a hammer. The Red Hand was standing, waiting. The steel gauntlet was thrust out, the fingers and thumb brutally spread to clamp down....

"Yes," the Red Hand murmured, *"close your mouth!"*

Nita shut her eyes, but she could not stop her ears, for her hands still were bound behind her. She heard the gibbering screams mount to an incredible crescendo, then become suddenly muffled. They were broken by a rending groan, a scrambling of undirected feet on the concrete floor and then they burst forth again. Before there had been abject terror; now there was shriek on shriek of unutterable pain and once more that beating, beating sound of feet that moved convulsively; queer bubbling words that were formless and yet were words. Nita stiffened as the harsh, mocking voice of the Red Hand spoke again in her ear.

"You ladies will open your eyes," it said, "or they will be opened for you—*by the Red Hand!*"

Nita bit her lips. She heard Bubbles shriek and her eyes flew open. But it was only that Bubbles had opened her eyes and seen. Bubbles slid to the floor in a faint.

"I'm afraid you'll have to look, too," the Red Hand said beside Nita.

Nita looked. She looked, and the basement tilted crazily and her knees turned to rubber beneath her.

She said slowly, harshly, "You are a fiend!"

The Red Hand chuckled. His hollow, muffled laughter rang up to the ceiling, beat back from the walls and through it. With a moan, Nita sank to the ground. She thought, *this was how Laskar died!* It seemed hours before the screams of the maimed Sharps ceased to ring through the basement, but finally they were stilled. The Red Hand still chuckled.

"Now then, ladies," he said. "Have you quite recovered, Miss Morval? Yes. Then, listen carefully. I have promised you a certain reward, Miss Morval, if you perform my orders faithfully. You have seen what happens to those who fail me. Yes, yes. You have seen—and *heard*. All right now. Get out—and remember!" Bubbles Morval left hurriedly and the Red Hand turned to Nita.

"But you… You are different. A spy perhaps. And for spies, there is a cure." The steel gauntlet moved toward Nita's face!

CHAPTER 7
WANTED—KILLERS

HAD WENTWORTH guessed Nita's presence in Balmy's, or known that it was the Red Hand who challenged him through the door of Balmy's office, not even imminent death would have driven him away. But he could not know—and the Spider had learned at least a part of what he had sought. He laughed down at the trembling Sharps, from whom terror had shaken the last dregs of information, then he stepped into the closet in Balmy's office, manipulated the pivot door in its back—and was gone.

A few minutes later he had mounted to the roof. Sharps had known little enough, but he had revealed how the Red Hand had organized the underworld, and he knew the Red Hand's go-between, a little rat of a man known satirically as Big Johnny Gaynor. Tomorrow, the Spider would have to pay a visit to Big Johnny Gaynor. Meantime, the gray light was brightening in the East. Yes, the Spider must flee to cover.

It was Blinky McQuade once more who slipped from a tenement a half dozen doors from Balmy's, who stopped presently at an all-night restaurant that had a dial telephone in a booth. From it, Wentworth called his home for word of Nita. She still had not returned. God, was it possible that after all she had been taken a prisoner at Balmy's?

He raced back but the place was deserted. This was madness, he told himself. He could not have passed so close to Nita and not known her. She could not have been at Balmy's. So he told himself, but he was terribly shaken. If she had fallen into the power of the Red Hand! It would be hours now before he could act. It was far too early for Blinky McQuade to call on Big Johnny Gaynor. The Spider could not walk by daylight—and no lesser power could force the truth from those upon whom the blight of the Red Hand had fallen.

IT WAS scarcely nine o'clock when Blinky McQuade shuffled out into the dim sunlight of the slums, able to bear the inactivity no longer. He was a shuffling, unkempt figure as he made his way through the slattern streets, hat drawn far down to shield his eyes against the glare. His spectacles fitted closely and arched green hoods projected over each lens like an anti-glare shield of the old-type automobile headlight. Despite all that, his forehead was perpetually wrinkled with strain. Scarcely daring to hope, he made his way again to a telephone, but the answer was the same. Nita was missing....

Early as it was for denizens of the underworld to be abroad, Wentworth found that Big Johnny Gaynor's office, rigged up like a huge employment agency, was jammed with men and a scattering of women. He could identify known pickpockets, *heist* men, a few of the old-time racket killers; grifters of all kinds; a half dozen safe crackers; a score of others who bore the prison mark, game for any crime from robbery to kidnapping—or murder. And the sight shook Wentworth as not even the fire in the theater had done. No need to ask why they were here.

The criminals of the city were turning out as one man to join the union of the Red Hand!

A few of the waiting men grumbled greetings at Blinky and he wrinkled up his forehead as if he must strain his eyes to identify them.

"Can't see a damned thing in all this light," he complained. "Hell of a time of day to have to go out. This damned Red Hand…."

Silence fell sharply and men shuffled almost frantically away from him. Under the hoods of his glasses, his eyes darted keenly over the crowd. They were as frightened as if he had uttered blasphemy against a vengeful and omnipresent god! Wentworth chattered on….

"I go to China Sam's and can't get in without a ticket," he said. "I go to Balmy's and Sharps gives me the bum's rush!"

"Pipe down, Blinky," a man whispered in his ear. "Pipe down—or you may get what Sharps got!"

Wentworth's mind grasped at the name. Sharps? Had the fool revealed then what he had told the Spider?

"Yeah?" Wentworth's brows contracted. "I don't know what he got, but I'm tickled silly."

"The Red Hand!" the man whispered. "The Red Hand is what he got—right across the face!"

Wentworth made his shoulders shudder and fell respectfully quiet. Sharps had been suspected of talking to the Spider—and death under the Red Hand was his penalty! Before long, they would fear this Red Hand more than the Spider's swift vengeance. He would have to work fast, or there would be no stopping this incredible unionization of the underworld.

The Red Hand had hit on an insidious plan, according to Sharps. The first anyone had known about it was when six minor crooks, on one night, got messages signed with the Red Hand. Each message cased an easy job of robbery or burglary and several of the men, just out of prison and broke, had fallen for it. Their loot had been rich, and, following the orders of the Red Hand's slips, there had been no trouble at all.

From that small beginning, the Red Hand had gradually spread out. Crooks, losing their suspicions, fell over each other trying to get hold of one of the Red Hand's messages. And Balmy's was where most of them were given out.... The part that Wentworth could not understand was that the Red Hand apparently got nothing at all out of the deal!

It was with difficulty that Wentworth drove his mind to these general thoughts. He was harassed with worries about Nita. No chance that she was concealed in this loft building, of course. If she had been identified, she would be the personal prisoner of the Red Hand by now and only one thing would avail! The Spider must learn the identity of the Red Hand at once... A bitter smile twisted Wentworth's lips at the thoughts. As easy as that! But it had to be done.

IT WAS two hours before Blinky McQuade's name was called by the clerk to whom he had identified himself. Wentworth deliberately stumbled against the railing instead of the gate and had to be led through it to the door behind which Big Johnny

Gaynor had his office. Gaynor was tipped back, his round head cocked at a condescending angle, a black cigar in his mouth.

"Well, Blinky," he rasped in his high, unpleasant voice. "What can we do for you?"

Blinky McQuade peered about and located a chair, eased into it. "I can't get in nowhere no more withouten I get a card from the Red Hand," he complained, "but what I'm after is some of this easy sugar lying around. What do I have to do to sign up?"

Big Johnny stood up. It made him very little taller than when he sat. "You're blind as a bat, Blinky," he said harshly. "You ain't no good to a big shot like the Red Hand."

Blinky grinned mirthlessly. "I don't open safes with my eyes, Johnny. And I don't make noise like a piteman. And after dark, I can see like a cat!"

Big Johnny stood staring at him, hands locked behind him under his coat, scowling above his big black cigar. "Like a cat, huh?" He sat down abruptly and picked up a batch of papers,

shuffling through them. Wentworth twisted a little so that he had a clear view, lifted one hand as if to shield his eyes from the light. Actually, he adjusted to a fine focus the left lens of his spectacles which was a double glass.

He sucked in his breath softly, as through the lens he got the gist of several of the papers lying loosely on the desk. It wasn't possible to read them closely but he could read enough. That top one listed the men needed for "Job 4—Three good gunmen, armed; a get-away driver with hot car; woman for lookout." He peered farther and found "Job 5—expert safecracker, not peteman, driving own car." As coolly as that, the Red Hand stated his criminal employment needs!

Big Johnny grunted. "Maybe we can use you, McQuade," he said shortly. "Run along home and if we can, you'll get a message."

Wentworth got heavily to his feet. "Yeah, and what about me getting into Balmy's or China Sam's? A guy can't even buy a drink."

Big Johnny laughed. "Run on home, McQuade."

"Geez," Wentworth grumbled admiringly, "The Red Hand must have the law sewed up as tight as he has us to get away with running an office like this!"

"Tighter!" Big Johnny grinned. "Look out, that ain't the door. That's a bookcase!"

Blinky growled a curse, swung all the way around and saw Johnny putting the papers into a compartment hollowed out of the desktop itself and entered through a narrow slide in the edge of what seemed solid wood. So that was it! Ostensibly, this was an employment agency. If police searched the office, they would find nothing criminal because it would be concealed in that clever hiding place. He had seen it because he was supposed to be blind as a bat in daylight.

WENTWORTH FORCED himself to remain in McQuade's room and laid his plans. If the Red Hand failed to assign him to a job tonight, thus giving him an entree into the gang itself, he would rob Gaynor's office of its lists of "jobs." He might also find the names of the men assigned to those jobs and be able to tip off the police. Wholesale arrests would help shake the faith of the underworld in this Red Hand. But that was a long chance. Let him once learn how the detailed messages from the Red Hand were distributed....

Wentworth jerked out of a sound sleep to find darkness thick in his room. He cursed raggedly, swung his feet to the floor— and sat staring. There, where a slit of yellow light showed under the door was a white square, an envelope! He could not repress a tremor in his hand as he snatched it up. He had no doubt what this was... but fatigue and sleep had wrecked his plans. He did not know how the message had been delivered... He ripped open the envelope. The sight of the blood-red cruel signature stabbed like a knife. It was this that had heralded Laskar's death, that now held Nita in its power.

Slowly, he read the words and a hard smile formed on his lips. It was still all right then. The message read:—

Go to Balmy's tonight for instructions. This will admit you.

Subconsciously, Wentworth noted that the message was

merely typewritten, that the machine used was an L.C. Smith, pica type. It was easy to determine that by distinctive variations in the fonts used. Carefully, he folded the paper—and a violent blow smashed the flimsy lock on the door, slammed it inward. A man came bounding into the room with a stubby revolver clutched ready in his fist. It was the Morval girl's fiancé, Don Blaine! Wentworth's gun hand already had jerked up, but he checked it, pretended to cringe.

"Where is she?" Blaine demanded hoarsely. "Damn you, tell me where she is, or...."

He seized Wentworth's coat lapels in a powerful fist and Wentworth let him do it.

"What the hell's the matter with you?" he snarled back at Blaine. "Think I'm the kind of punk that chases dames?" He could see that Blaine was frantic with concern. It was plain that Blaine meant Bubbles Morval had come to deliver the message from the Red Hand. She had lied to him then about her reasons for being in Balmy's Bit House... But, hell, Blaine also was bodyguard to Clare Sutton! Perhaps it was she he meant....

Blaine flung McQuade backward on the bed, stood over him with the gun poised for a blow. "You'll talk, damn you," he whispered. "She came here to bring you a message from Ransome, and she hasn't come out."

Wentworth made his voice a whine. "I ain't got no deal with Ransome. Who in the hell are you talking about? Listen there's more than one way of getting out of here. Why blame me because a dame gives you the slip?"

Another idea had glanced across Wentworth's mind. There

was a chance that Blaine also was in with the Red Hand, and that this whole thing was a test to see whether Blinky McQuade would talk about his message from the Red Hand. That "message from Ransome" made it almost certain that Blaine meant Bubbles Morval as the girl. Did it mean also that Ransome was the Red Hand—or did Bubbles have some reason for lying to Blaine?

With a jerk of his muscles that he could scarcely conceal, Wentworth remembered suddenly that the Red Hand message had been typed on a Smith machine—and that all the machines in Ransome's office were of that make! Subconsciously, he fingered the message which he had been forced to conceal in his hand when Blaine burst in. Like a cat, Blaine pounced forward, twisted open his hand.

"I knew you lied!" Blaine panted out. "She was here! Now by God, you'll talk or—or I'll blow your guts out!"

His eyes were stretched round, as hard and glittering as agate marbles and Wentworth saw with a sense of deadly peril that Blaine was beyond reason—that he would really shoot!

CHAPTER 8
THE SPIDER WALKS AGAIN

IN PLAYING out the role of Blinky McQuade, Wentworth had allowed himself to be man-handled by Blaine. As a consequence, he had been forced into an extremely perilous position—flat on his back on the bed, with Blaine's gun pointed at his heart and Blaine's fear-crazed eyes glaring into his. And

Blaine was too experienced to stand where Wentworth's feet could strike him. It might be possible to distract his attention momentarily and shoot—but the Spider did not harm the innocent, and he was increasingly convinced that Blaine was in the clear.

"All right. All right!" he whined up at Blaine in Blinky McQuade's rasping voice. "I'll tell you all I know." He started to sit up. Blaine's gun stopped him. Blaine was going to be hard to take.

"That note," Wentworth pointed to the message from the Red Hand which Blaine had seized, "will maybe tell you where to find the girlfriend. I ain't read it yet."

Blaine snatched the paper, backed the width of the room.

"You stay right where you are, McQuade," he ordered. He jerked his eyes to the note, quickly looked back to the bed. Wentworth had not moved. Blaine relaxed a little, put his eyes back on the note—and Wentworth heaved the bed pillow.

To Wentworth, the pillow seemed to float like a feather. No weight in it and no impact, but momentarily it would blind Blaine. With the swing of his arm, Wentworth rolled. The gun smashed out. He saw the pillow jerk and felt the bullet fan past his throat. He slid sideways to the floor and hit on his knees. Blaine struck furiously at the pillow, and Wentworth launched himself across the room in a low headlong dive.

His straining fingers closed over one ankle. He hugged it to him. His shoulders hit only the wall, but he carried Blaine's foot with him. Blaine wheeled wildly, trying to maintain a one-legged balance, hit the floor hard.

With a curse that was almost a sob of thankfulness, Wentworth made another dive from his knees, driving a right under Blaine's chin while his left grappled for the gun. He slung in two more blows before he realized the man was knocked out, then scrambled panting to his feet, recovered the Red Hand message and his glasses, saved from damage by the stout hoods. Then he stood for a moment staring down at Blaine.

Blaine's tawny hair was sprawled over his forehead, his arms flung up like a child's in sleep. With his eyes closed, the taut man-muscles of his cheeks relaxed, he was strangely appealing. Wentworth shook his head. Blaine might be innocent, but he could no longer believe in the honesty of Bubbles Morval. It seemed her typewriter had written the criminal summonses of the Red Hand!

With a long stride, Wentworth reached the panel in the foot of the bed, and from behind it snatched out the cape and black hat of the Spider, the few simple factors of disguise which would change Blinky McQuade into that dread nemesis of the night. For the Spider must walk again!

Swiftly, Wentworth stowed the garments about his person, cape and crushable hat folded flat beneath his vest. Then he dragged Blaine into the hallway. He would recover consciousness, but if police should come first, they would not find him in Blinky McQuade's room.

A FEW minutes later, Wentworth was shambling through the dark streets on his way to Balmy's but he was still Blinky McQuade. Before the Spider could take the trail tonight, McQuade must answer the summons of the Red Hand! It was a block from Balmy's that Wentworth's ever-questing eyes brought him to a dead stop. He was staring at a coupé he recognized, one of the three he kept for emergency in the garages near his apartment house. With a cautious glance along the night-darkened street, he sidled up to the car. On the handle of the locked door were two police tickets issued for parking. One had been attached the night before… *The night before!* God, there no longer was any doubt. Nita had driven this car here and, from its location, she had gone to Balmy's. She had been there last night when the Spider made his raid!

That knowledge shook Wentworth as had nothing else in his battle with the Red Hand. Like all men who live on the fringes of death, he had learned to depend on intuition in time of hazard. That had failed him. Within a few yards—possibly a few feet of Nita, he had been unaware of her proximity. Now, she was a captive of the Red Hand. But where—where?

It was Balmy himself who opened the door for Blinky McQuade tonight and, from behind the disguising spectacles, Wentworth's eyes stabbed deep. Here was one of those who had helped capture Nita! Wentworth fought down his anger. Balmy was only a pawn, as Bubbles Morval and Blinky McQuade were pawns in this fierce game of murder and loot. Only one thing would avail Wentworth now—the death of the Red Hand.

In all the main bar room of Balmy's, there was tension, a louder raucous note in men's voices, a shriller tone in the laughter of the few women. Wentworth moved with McQuade's grumpy manner to a table, alone. He was not surprised when, ten minutes later, a darkly pert girl, as out of place here as a police uniform, entered the main room: Bubbles Morval. Her eyes skipped over the crowd, rested briefly on him. A whispering silence fell upon the room. Bubbles paid it no heed, but moved directly to Blinky's table. Her mouth was drawn, the light in her eyes almost feverish. Beneath the table, her hand touched Wentworth's knee. When his hand went down, she passed him a folded sheet of paper, and a few minutes later, without having spoken, arose and walked on.

Blinky McQuade also moved toward the hall and the street, conscious of the envious eyes of the assemblage because he had received an assignment from the Red Hand. As he entered the hall, he found Balmy bending over a man, unconscious on the floor.

Balmy looked up with a crooked grin. "This punk tried to crash the door, the damned fool!"

He rolled the man over. It was Don Blaine!

Apparently, the ex-detective had read at least part of the note, or else accidentally had picked up Bubbles' trail. Wentworth hesitated, then stepped over the body. If he could not spare time to hunt for Nita, he could not hope to rescue Blaine now… Probably he would only be held prisoner. *He* did not have the misfortune to be a friend of the Spider!

WENTWORTH READ the second message of the Red Hand in a telephone booth. It told him simply that if he would crack the safe in the cashier's cage at the Grand Avenue Bus Company offices just off Riverside Drive Viaduct, he would get away with more than twenty thousand dollars! The instructions gave a complete picture of the office, the number of watchmen and their positions, told him the place to park his car and the best getaway route—down Riverside Drive. A slight tremor seized Wentworth's hands. No wonder the underworld flocked to the banner of the Red Hand! Not once in a hundred times did a criminal have such a complete picture of the place he planned to rob! The message finished:

> … Two of the watchmen will be out of the way at eleven-thirty. That is when you must strike. Fail us at your peril.

When Wentworth left the booth, he had already determined to commit the robbery. He could cache the money and return it later, but right now it was imperative that he cement himself in the Red Hand's organization. Yes, he would rob the safe, but first—Ransome's office.

It was Blinky McQuade who rented a Drive-Yourself car and sped northward and westward toward the Electra Building; who forced a door on a dark court beside the building. But it was the Spider who climbed the dim-lighted fire stairs to the twentieth floor.

There, Wentworth went at once to the typewriter in Ransome's outer office. Swiftly, his gloved hands glided over the keys, duplicating the message of the Red Hand by the light of a small desk lamp. Then he donned the glasses of Blinky McQuade and used the magnifying lens. As he studied the two papers side by side, his lips drew into a harsh gash. That *a* slightly above the line, that *o* slightly flattened on the lower right, the *n* below the line. There could be no doubt. The messages of the Red Hand had been written on this machine!

By heavens, this discovery was more important than a mere bit of evidence. If McQuade's instructions had been written here, so must orders for other criminals! Somewhere here there must be duplicates of those orders. Probably in the safe. Before he began opening that, he must eliminate all other sources. He jerked open drawers in Bubbles' desk, took out a series of shorthand notebooks and scanned the phonetic symbols. Pitman system, but with the individual variations all stenographers develop, peculiarities which make it practically impossible for one person to read another's work. Wentworth sprang to a filing cabinet. It was a work of moments to locate a letter which matched with notes in the book, and, with that as a key, to decipher Bubbles' shorthand notes. Wentworth scanned through three books, picking only a sentence here and there, conscious of the fleeting minutes. In the fourth book he found what he sought—the very message he had in his pocket!

WENTWORTH WAS elated and worried. If there were other messages here besides his own, he could tip off the police and disrupt the night's plans of the Red Hand. But the very openness with which the book was left here augured against the guilt of Ransome. He searched the drawers of the desk more thoroughly and, under old papers, found the culminating piece of evidence. A rubber stamp to imprint the signature of the Red Hand! Resolutely, Wentworth closed his mind to puzzlement over the meaning of his discoveries. That must come later. Right now, he must translate these notes, discover what other crimes the Red Hand planned for this night. At eleven-thirty, Blinky

McQuade must rob a safe. He glanced at his watch. Quarter of eleven....

More and more rapidly as Wentworth became accustomed to Bubbles' notes, the messages began to unfold. As he worked, a fury was born within him. The thing was damnable! Every crime planned for the night was concentrated on the city's bus companies. Five other safe robberies were planned; three holdups of payrolls for the night-shift drivers. The fare-collection offices were to be looted, and everywhere the instructions were minute, the mapping of the territory and guards, even the getaway charts were perfectly planned! Each job was numbered, and... Wentworth's head whipped toward the door of the office. He had heard a furtive foot-step! With a movement quick and light as a shadow, Wentworth was behind the desk with the compact weight of an automatic nestled in his hand.

The footsteps came swiftly to the door and paused there. Except for the desk lamp, the office was in darkness and he could see the vague shadow outline of someone standing there in the hall, silhouetted on the ground glass by the corridor light. By God, a woman! Wentworth smiled grimly as he went to the door with long, silent strides. So Bubbles Morval had come back!

His gloved hand closed about the knob and, with a wrench he flung the door wide, threw his arms about the woman.

"Silence!" he ordered fiercely. "Silence! The Spider orders it!"

For a space of heartbeats, the woman stood rigid in his arms while he realized that she was too tall for Bubbles Morval, and that her uncovered hair caught vagrant beams of light like tarnished red gold. With an exclamation, he whirled her inside the office and shut the door.

"Clare Sutton!" he cried softly.

For once, the girl's heavy-lidded eyes were wide. Her breath came shudderingly.

"You… frightened me," she stammered. "You…" She bowed her face and sagged into a chair. When, presently she lifted her head again there was a faint smile on her lips. "I'm sorry," she said, "I'm better now. Thank God, I've found you here! Today my father received an order from the Red Hand!"

"*Your father!*" Wentworth was startled.

"Yes. He has a brokerage office in Wall Street. The Red Hand ordered him to sell short the stocks of all the bus companies in the city. He got a message signed with a red fist… Oh, a horrible fist!"

Wentworth uttered a low exclamation. Sutton was ordered to sell bus stocks short, and tonight there would be a score of crimes striking at bus companies….

BUT WHAT possible connection could this revelation have with Clare Sutton's presence here? He asked her that drily, and Clare flushed.

"I always thought that Mr. Ransome hated my father," she said quietly. "They're always together, but if you could see the way Ransome looks at him! When Dad got this note, he called Ransome, and Ransome said he had one, too. Said he thought it unimportant and had thrown it in his desk or somewhere. I came to find out if he told the truth!"

There was a scarcely perceptible change in Clare's voice and Wentworth was convinced this last was a lie.

"Why did you go to Laskar's office yesterday?" Wentworth asked abruptly.

Clare Sutton's eyes jerked to his. She opened her lips, then hesitated.

"Don Blaine," Wentworth urged, "is a prisoner of the Red Hand!"

A sharp cry forced itself from Clare's lips before she crushed it back with her hands.

"There's no use lying to me as you did to the police," he said harshly. "I know you had no account with Laskar. Why did you go there?"

Her eyes would not meet his. "Be careful," Wentworth warned. "I know more than you think. I know that it was because you went to Laskar that he was killed. And I know—" He whirled her about, and with a fierce slash of his hand, ripped the silk of her dress. The white flesh was lacerated with welts, hideously bruised. "I know that you were flogged!"

Clare Sutton sagged to her knees. "My father," she stammered. "He... he loses his head sometimes, but...."

"You came here tonight to help your father," Wentworth said shortly. "You went to Laskar to help your father, so he flogged you!"

"He doesn't understand," Clare pleaded. "He was afraid of what would happen. Afraid of what you might do! I swear this is the truth!"

Impatiently, Wentworth looked again at his watch. Good

God, there was no time to be lost! In twenty minutes, Blinky McQuade must be robbing a bus company safe, and the police had not been warned of the other crimes that impended. He was convinced he had not yet got the truth from Clare Sutton, unless—*unless her father was the Red Hand!*

By God, it fitted that way! Ransome's hatred might easily be a reflection of Sutton's dislike. All these maneuvers involving Ransome's office bore more the look of a frame-up than actual guilt. And Sutton employed nothing but "reformed" criminals! If he had learned Clare had gone to see Laskar, he might have flogged her.

HE SAID, slowly, "I suppose Don Blaine can confirm what you said to Laskar?" He waited for her words.

Clare shook her head, "He waited outside in the car."

Wentworth leaned toward her. "I suppose you know Blaine had nothing to do with your being robbed of your jewels, as you told Kirkpatrick—that is, if you were robbed. Don Blaine was in this office at the time with the girl he loves, Bubbles Morval."

Anger darkened Clare's face. "That little tramp! Bubbles is two-timing Donald and I told him so. She's stepping out with Ransome."

"How do you know?" Wentworth demanded. If that were so, it might be additional evidence against Ransome.

Clare shrugged. "I know. She's the type!"

Wentworth turned angrily away. There was no truth in the woman. He whipped out from a pocket in his cape the silken "web" and with a few deft movements bound Clare Sutton to a chair. She stared up into his face with haunted, frightened eyes. He would have to leave her here until he had performed the errand of the Red Hand. By that time, perhaps, she would be willing to talk!

Rapidly, Wentworth dialed police headquarters, got Kirkpatrick on the phone. "Kirkpatrick," he said in the dry, flat voice of the Spider, "I am about to tell you how to smash the men of the Red Hand. If you think it is more important to capture me, by all means trace this call. Listen...."

Job No. 4 Wentworth mentioned last.

"The lookout on this job," he mentioned, "will be a woman."

Without another word to Clare Sutton, Wentworth sped from the office. Already, he had lost too much time. He would have to drive like the wind to keep his rendezvous with crime. Of necessity, he had tipped the police to his own crime also, but he had falsified the time. He had no alternative there. If he alone, out of the entire night's list of crimes, went unspotted by the police, the Red Hand might find it necessary to probe more deeply into the identity of Blinky McQuade! He could only hope that the police would not set their trap for Blinky too early....

CHAPTER 9
JOB NO. 5

MANY TIMES in the Spider's battles, Nita van Sloan had faced a hideous death, but here in this murder basement, threatened by that steel gauntlet which had just killed a man so horribly, Nita felt a scream push irresistibly from her throat.

"Don't be afraid." The man who wore the mask of the Red Hand was chuckling again. *"The glove* doesn't have to kill you. It all depends on whether I wish to be merciful. I could merely... *slap your face!"*

With a fierce effort, Nita regained control of herself.

"Geez, chief," she put admiration into her voice. "You're a wonder! Could I go for a big shot like you! But listen...."

The masked face was just above hers and she could see the cold glitter of the eyes. She kept her gaze away from the gauntlet.

"Listen," she hurried on, "all I wanted was to get in Balmy's and maybe meet up with a friend. I'd seen the Morval dame in a lawyer's office and so I used her name when Balmy told me off. That's all. Listen, you give me a job to do, any kind of a job. Try me out, see."

Nita fairly held her breath while the Red Hand hovered over her. Finally, the man grunted and stepped back.

"That might be an idea," he said. Presently, he left.

It was hours later that there came two men who grinned at her with sly eyes and lingered needlessly over loosening the bonds from about her body.

"Better lay off," one rasped at the other. "The chief's got his eye on this dame."

Nita felt her flesh contract at the man's words, but her sauntering gait as she mounted the steps after the blood had crept painfully back to her cramped limbs, her gestures as she smoothed the dress over her hips were still those of an underworld moll.

Her ultimate safety lay, she knew, in preserving her disguise. She was thrust alone into an office. Two men waited for her, the Red Hand and a small, ratty-looking man with a big cigar.

"I've been thinking over you doing a job for me," the Red Hand began at once. "Job Number Four calls for a woman lookout. It's a payroll stickup. You game?"

Hope leaped up in Nita's breast. She nodded eagerly. "Just try me!"

"I think I shall," the Red Hand said softly. "Remember! If you fail on your job, *the glove* waits for you!"

Nita could only repeat, "Try me and see!"

HER MIND was already racing with hope of escape, but more than that with plans for snaring the criminals with whom she would work. It was typical of her that she should thus think of furthering Dick Wentworth's work even before her own safety.

The Red Hand sent Nita out with the two men, then he chuckled. He leaned back and laughed loudly. The little man shifted nervously on his seat, rolled the cigar between his lips.

"You're all wet this time, chief," he said raspingly. "The dame's fixing to double-cross us sure as hell."

The Red Hand rested his gauntlet on the desk. "Just so, Johnny. But you've realized by now who she is, haven't you? Surely, my lad, you recall the Spider crashed into Balmy's to find her? That makes it clearer. She is Nita van Sloan. I had the numbers checked on that gun we took away from her."

Johnny stared.

Chuckling again, the Red Hand opened a drawer and picked up an automatic. "Here is the automatic Sharps took from Miss van Sloan, Johnny. It's licensed and registered in her name as I said. On Job Four, make sure somebody is murdered. It doesn't matter much whom. A policeman? Very good... but make sure he is killed *with this gun!* Then leave the gun behind and have one of our boys knock out the woman and leave her there, too... My, oh my, the Spider is just going to love what we do with Nita van Sloan! We'll have her in as neat a murder frame as the one we built for Dick Wentworth...."

FOR A moment, both men were silent. Slowly, the Red Hand nodded again. "Do the same thing for this chap, Blaine. We have his gun. Use it on Job Seven, then bring it back. Any time we need to, we can send that gun to the police and he'll be framed cold for murder. Well, what are you waiting for, Johnny?"

"Nothing! Nothing!" Big Johnny stammered. He jumped to his feet and his short-striding legs carried him choppily out the door... It was five minutes later that a puzzled gunman entered with a card that bore only the stamp of a red fist upon it.

"Dame downstairs, chief," he said "Says you'd better see her right away."

The Red Hand jerked to his feet. "Very well," he said softly. "Show her in."

It was Clare Sutton who came in, alone.

"Ugh," she said, "the mask again."

The Red Hand came around the desk, "I told you not to come here, Clare," he said coldly. "Is it possible you want another beating?"

Clare said savagely, "You're mighty sure I won't talk, damn you! Listen, you've got Don Blaine a prisoner here. I want you

99

to turn him loose. At once. Or I'm going to the Spider with what I know!"

The gauntlet reached out slowly for her face. Clare Sutton stood rigid against the threat of that horror until it almost touched her flesh, then she sobbed and winced aside.

"I wouldn't have to kill you," he said. "I could release the acid without using the poison needle!"

"I mean it!" Clare cried desperately. "You dare not hurt me!"

The Red Hand shook his head. "My dear, you are wrong. I'll admit I wouldn't kill you. After all a man must have some decency with his relations...."

"You beast!"

"But that doesn't keep me from punishing you as you deserve," the Red Hand went on smoothly. "I have the whip here in my desk...."

Clare dropped to her knees. "Oh, in heaven's name, not that!" she gasped. "But you don't want Blaine. What could you want with him? I haven't talked. I'm not going to!"

"Exactly, my dear! For if you do... your dear Donald Blaine is going to get the gauntlet across his face! Probably I won't kill him. I'll let him go on living—for your sake, Clare. You see I know all about your philandering!" He leaned toward her. "How would you like to kiss Donald... after *the glove!*"

Clare looked sick. She turned toward the door.

"Just a minute, Clare," said the Red Hand. "How did you know Blaine was a prisoner here?"

Clare said swiftly. "I couldn't find him. I guessed!"

The Red Hand said nothing and Clare came forward with quick steps. "You must believe me. I guessed!"

The Red Hand opened a drawer and took out a coiled whip of braided leather. Clare shrieked and ran to the door. It was locked.

"I don't like to be lied to, Clare," the Red Hand said softly. "You may as well confess. You have been talking with… the Spider! Damn your double-crossing soul. You've been talking with the Spider." The whip whistled, thudded in flesh.

"*God!*" she whimpered. "I can't stand the whip again. You're right. I've been talking with the Spider, but I didn't tell him anything. Not a thing! And I didn't go to him. He was already at Ransome's office when I got there."

Clare told the Red Hand, then, everything that had happened in Ransome's office, how a watchman had found and freed her after the Spider had left. When she finished, the Red Hand knocked her flat on the floor. Afterward, he wielded the whip. When he stopped, he was panting and Clare was unconscious. The Red Hand shouted through the halls for Big Johnny Gaynor.

"Don't bother to frame Nita van Sloan," he said violently. "Kill her! And see that instructions for the job, signed with *the glove*, are on her body. That will stop the police from working with the Spider. By God, I'll smash him. I'll… I'll…" He reached out with the gauntlet and gripped the face of a man who stood nearby. He lifted the man off his feet, held him that way while the man's eyes bulged, while his fists beat futilely and his screams fluttered against the palm of that brutal, unyielding gauntlet.

101

"Just like that," whispered the Red Hand, "I'll crush him!" He threw the dying man to the floor, spun on his heel and stalked out. His laughter began deep in his chest and bubbled up behind his mask, swelled until it reverberated through the vast, empty, reechoing halls.

"Just... like... that!" he whispered again.

CHAPTER 10
DEATH ON THE VIADUCT

IT WAS not the Spider, but Blinky McQuade, who went deftly about the looting of the Grand Avenue bus company safe. He had found the plans of the Red Hand accurate in every detail and the police, swamped by a score of other calls, had not yet come to guard this place. Nevertheless, it was drawing close to midnight—the time Wentworth had given Kirkpatrick as zero hour for this robbery—when the safe finally yielded to McQuade's sensitive manipulation.

Quickly, he stripped the strong box, thrust the packets of bills into a bag, and slipped hurriedly back to the doorway beside which lay the watchman he had been forced to knock out. He stood there to study the street. If the police had arrived while he was inside, he would be trapped. There were three cars parked nearby, two belonging to the watchmen and his own rented coupé.

Abruptly, he stooped over the watchman and stripped off his long uniform coat and cap, rapidly donned them. He put the bag of loot inside his belt, buttoned the coat over it so that he appeared to be a paunched older man. He unlocked the door, stepped out and lighted a cigarette, stood there smoking for a few moments, then began to pace slowly up and down. If the police were watching, apparently they were not yet suspicious of him.

Wentworth finished the cigarette, tossed it aside and began to feel his pockets. With a shrug, he walked toward the parked cars. He was sure now that he was watched. The black pit of that doorway across the street held a shadow that was alive. But there was no challenge as he leaned into his rented coupé and turned on the dome light, elaborately searched the dashboard compartments. He cursed, got under the wheel and kicked the starter....

"Hey, you, watchman!" The hail came from across the street.

Wentworth kept the starter going until the engine caught, didn't look around until a uniformed figure holding a riot-gun stepped out of the shadows.

"Hey!" Wentworth gasped. "Who are you?"

"Police." The man walked nearer. "Where do you think you're going?"

"What's it to you?"

The officer was near at hand now, but Wentworth's face was shadowed by the visor of the watchman's cap. He met the stare steadily.

The cop nodded. "Had a tip-off crooks were going to take your safe tonight. Better go back inside!"

Wentworth said, "Hell you have! Geez, I just ran out of cigarettes and was going to get some. You ain't got none, I

The careening bus tossed the car through the guard rail.

guess." The cop grinned a little. He moved forward, riot-gun sagging over his arm, pulling out a pack of cigarettes.

"I know how it is when you want a smoke," he said.

Wentworth's hand vised shut on the cop's wrist instead of his cigarettes. A gun popped into his other fist. "Get on the running board and keep your mouth shut," he whispered, "or I'll blow you wide open!"

THE COP'S mouth sagged open and Wentworth whipped him up against the car, used his feet to accelerate and let out the clutch. The car leaped forward, slamming the officer to the running board, hammering the riot-gun from his hand. Wentworth let his automatic drop into his lap to handle the wheel. Shouts ripped out behind him, but as he had calculated, the police held their fire because of his prisoner. He hung on to the cursing officer until he had whirled a corner, braked long enough to strike through the open window with his doubled fist, then let the man slide to the pavement. Instantly, Wentworth was roaring off.

They'd have a car to pursue all right, but if he could increase his lead a little, he could discard the uniform and become Blinky McQuade again. He had traveled three blocks before he heard a police car's siren rip out behind him. He glimpsed the dark opening of a warehouse loading platform, swung into the arched gateway. Instantly, he was out of the car, ripping off the uniform coat and cap. He hesitated over the Spider disguise, then thrust it under his vest and, carrying the bag of loot, he hurried off.

Useless to hope that the police would not search and question him if they saw him. But around the corner the Riverside

Drive viaduct rose high against the sky. The pillars were steel on concrete buttresses. A seventy-five foot climb up one of those would put him on the viaduct itself. He could ride downtown in a bus of the very company he had robbed, the last thing the police would expect....

Without being spotted by the police, he reached one of the pillars, thrust the money inside his coat and sprang to the concrete base, went up rapidly.

Then, when the viaduct was momentarily empty of cars, he swiftly mounted the guard railing. Gasping for breath, his muscles aching, he was on the bridge itself. Slowly he shambled toward its northern end to wait for a downtown bus. They would be crowded tonight. Even so late as this, many people would be riding the upper decks to enjoy the soft air of this summer night. WENTWORTH WAS compelled to let two buses pass before one arrived which could take another passenger. As he moved, with the shuffling, half-blind pace of Blinky McQuade to get on the rear platform, a man he had not noticed before darted from the shadows and leaped ahead of him. His shoulder brushed Wentworth, then pushed his way inside. The bus was a new type on which passengers entered by the rear platform, left by a door at the front. The man made straight for the forward end. Wentworth stood on the platform a moment, paying his fare while the bus picked up speed on the long non-stop run across the viaduct. On the upper deck, some young people were singing. Their voices made a soft sound on the night air.

Wentworth grinned at the conductor. "Grand to be young and take your girl for a bus ride," he said.

"Swell," the man agreed.

Wentworth stood listening to the singing. Perhaps it was the relaxation of danger, but his throat could choke over the beauty of youth singing together in the night. There had been little such beauty in his life—until he had met Nita.

And since then there had been so many bloody battles. *Nita!* He knew better how to search for her now. When he had disposed of this loot… He was gazing, without awareness, at the man who had got aboard when he had. Suddenly, his eyes came sharply to focus. The man was bending over the driver, and as Wentworth watched, he saw the man's right shoulder drop and lift again in a movement he had learned to identify. The man had drawn a gun!

Almost before the meaning of that movement penetrated Wentworth's mind, he heard a muffled blast, saw the driver's head, then his body wrench violently to the left. With a curse, Wentworth sprang inside the bus, snatching for his automatic. It was already too late. Even as the shot rang out, the killer had seized the wheel of the bus and wrenched it about. The lurching turn made the huge top-heavy double-decker heel far over. Wentworth, in the middle of a stride, was hurled violently against passengers on the side seat.

Men shouted wildly. On the upper deck, the singing changed to frantic screams. Wentworth was aware of a body plunging past the windows, catapulted by the lurch, heard a despairing cry that ended in a crunching thud as the body hit. All these things happened in the split-second of the turn. Then the bus straightened out—headed directly for the guard railing, for a seventy-five foot dive to the concrete paving far below! It needed no genius to guess this was the work of the Red Hand. A ghastly accident would send bus stocks crashing!

The gun was slamming again, up front there, coming nearer as Wentworth pushed to his knees. The killer was bolting for the back door and escape before the bus took the final plunge, throwing lead ahead of him to blast the passengers back into their seats out of his way. From the corners of his eyes, Wentworth saw the conductor hammered back by a bullet, his back arching terribly, his arms flying high as he went over the rear of the bus to the roadway. An automobile horn was making a noise like a hoarse scream.

Wentworth's left hand was wrapped over the back of the seat behind which he had fallen. His right hand still clenched the gun. Lead whimpered past his ear and behind him a woman uttered a choked gasp. Wentworth dragged himself up until his eyes came above the seat back and his automatic convulsed in his hand. The killer's head wrenched back between his shoulders. He lunged full-length into the aisle. His face bounced.

WENTWORTH DID not even see that. He had continued his upward surge and, with the same movement, hurled himself bodily down the aisle toward where the murdered driver lolled in his seat. An automobile horn ripped upward to a frantic shriek and Wentworth had a glimpse of gleaming black and chromium as a car tried to dodge between the careening bus and the guard rail. He saw the car rock crazily as its outer wheels took the curbing of the sidewalk, saw terribly strained white faces peering out of the car's windows. And all about him and above him were the incredible throat-ripping screams of people in the throes of mad panic.

The impact of the bus against that racing car hurled Wentworth to his knees just as he reached the driver's compartment. The sedan leaped upward and he had a flashing view of its understructure. White faces and chromium smeared out of his range of vision. The horn stopped sounding and the tinny slam of the collision, the thin tinkle of flying glass came to him strangely through all that human bedlam. All those things Wentworth saw and felt as he was hurled forward with the impact of the collision. But he did not fall blindly. His left hand stabbed at and found the brake pedal. His right snatched at the air lever that operated the front door, whose opening would automatically slam on brakes, too.

Wentworth felt the floor of the bus rise up to meet him, realized it was the careening leap as the bus took the curb of sidewalk. Five feet from the guard rail. Impossible to stop in that space. Impossible, even with modern air brakes which were beginning to take hold. And still Wentworth pushed home those braking levers while his body still surged with the force of his fall. Glass popped out of windshield and windows, making an absurdly delicate tinkling all about him.

Again that tinny slam of collision, a crumpling, ripping sound of torn metal, then a ringing stroke like the reverberations of a huge steel bell, an explosion of minor supports as the guard rail was ripped through. The check of that collision slid Wentworth on his stomach along the floor, drove his skull violently against the forward wall of the coach. The ringing anvil sounds, the snapping explosions of supports continued. There was a moment of sickening pause and then... the floor jerked away from Wentworth, slammed back against his chest and stomach. The front wheels had gone over the edge....

"Get back!" Wentworth shouted. "Get back on the tail. Hurry, for God's sake!"

Momentarily, some projection in the understructure was holding the bus. He twisted his head about and saw that people already had started a panic dash for the rear. There was a grinding jar beneath the bus and it slipped a foot farther forward. Men were leaping from the upper deck, girls dropping. He saw their bright dresses flash past the open door two feet from his head. There was another grinding, jarring slip and he was no longer looking at the smashed guard rail. The bus was jutting out over space as far as the driver's seat. He saw the bright-colored dress of another girl flash by and her scream went on and on, downward. He shuddered. Another slip like that, and... But he had to hold the brakes. If he released them, the friction of those back wheels would no longer grip the pavement. The drag of the forward weight would draw the whole bus somersaulting into the streets below....

ALMOST WITH a sense of detachment, Wentworth stared at the smashed guard rail. The rods of steel were bent outward like wire screening where a bullet has smacked through. A huge section of the five-inch pipe at its top was simply gone, popped out into space at the first collision. Wentworth was aware only of the thud of feet as more and more leaped from the upper deck, from the rear platform.

"The wounded lady!" Wentworth shouted over his shoulder. "The old one there. She's shot. Carry her out!"

He saw a man's white face turn back toward him, but that was all.

"The wounded woman!" Wentworth yelled at them. "Get her out!' He saw a boy, white-faced beneath a mop of blazing red hair, start over the back rail of the bus. The boy tried to grin, waved a hand. "I'll get her, sir. You better jump! She's going to somersault."

Wentworth looked out of the door again. Jump… Where? He would have time only to make a stumbling jump straight out. And straight out meant—straight down seventy-five feet as that girl had fallen!

"I got her!" the boy yelled. "Now *jump!*"

At his words, the boy leaped over the rear of the platform with the old woman in his arms. As if that had been the one ounce of misbalance needed, the rear of the bus began to lift. A hoarse cry rose in Wentworth's throat. It was now or never. Useless to attempt to race up the incline of that aisle, now sharply steepening. He must go out the doorway. He had one chance in a thousand. If he could seize one of those twisted rods that thrust out above the darkly empty space below.…

Leaning far out, Wentworth leaped—and the bus faded away beneath his feet. That split-second of delay had been too long. Instead of thrusting against a firm spring-board, he had pushed on a yielding surface. His leap was short! Wentworth's arms strained frantically ahead of him, reaching for that bent rod which alone could save him. Then his tense fingers closed around it.

His swing swept him perilously on, whipped his legs downward and up again. The rod bent to a steep angle.

With the last lift of his shock-numbed arms, Wentworth dragged himself along the rod toward the viaduct, hand over hand while his body dangled above space. Eager hands reached out for him, caught his wrists. Down below, there was a crashing fury of sound, as the bus hit.

Wentworth, wrists gripped from above, could not help staring down. He saw a half dozen shapeless dark forms… The Spider had saved most of those aboard the bus, but the Red Hand had nevertheless scored terribly. And Wentworth knew that this was not the only blow that had been struck this night!

He felt himself dragged to the safety of the viaduct. Faces shouted words at him, hands beat on his back and a woman bore down on her knees, snatching his clenched fist to her lips… And a police siren was shrieking its way across the viaduct God, he could not afford to be, like this, the cynosure of all eyes! The loot of the safe was thrust inside of his coat, almost spilling to the ground. The police car halted and its two officers came pelting toward the crowd!

CHAPTER 11
NITA'S HOUR STRIKES

I T WAS impossible for Wentworth to flee from the police, even if he could fight clear of the worshipping crowd. It would only attract attention to himself, make his arrest certain. He did the next best thing. He hurried to meet the officers.

"For God's sake!" he cried. "Phone for some ambulances!"

The officers skated to a halt and one spun back toward the car. "He's right," this man yelled at his companion. "You watch the break while I report."

Wentworth sprang to the running board. "There's an all-night garage on the viaduct!" he shouted.

The cop nodded, already jerking the car into motion. "Get in. Tell me about it!"

Wentworth obeyed and, making his voice breathless, gasped disconnected phrases about the accident. "I'm all in," he concluded. "I almost got carried over and some people hauled me up on the bridge." He made that an excuse for hanging back when the cop dashed to the telephone. As soon as the man was out of sight, he gassed the police car out of the garage and in the street, bore the accelerator to the floor. In five minutes, this district would be overrun with police.

There was a burning fury in Wentworth's heart. Once more the Red Hand had killed terribly, wantonly. By God, when finally the Spider met him face to face there would be an accounting for every death. The Spider swore it!

The big clock above the 125th Street ferry showed quarter past midnight. At half past, the men of the Red Hand would stage Job Number Four, their biggest payroll robbery, at the downtown pay-off offices of the Central Avenue Bus Company. The police had been warned, but it was just possible that the Red Hand himself would join in the most lucrative raid of the night.

Wentworth's lips pressed coldly against his teeth. He hoped so. He prayed so. For the Spider would keep that rendezvous, too!

Only once did Wentworth stop in his dash. He called Ram Singh to bring his heavy, bulletproof Daimler to a spot near the Central offices. As soon as possible he must abandon this police car… The big bell in the Metropolitan tower tolled half past twelve when Wentworth was still six blocks from the bus company offices. At this moment, according to the Red Hand's plan, three killers in the uniforms of bus drivers would enter the doors. Outside, a girl would be waiting for a "date," the lookout for the robbers. Wentworth had warned the police about her particularly. She would be the danger point outside… How could he know that the lookout would be Nita, that the infuriated Red Hand had ordered her slain in reprisal!

While he sped downtown, Wentworth had fumbled out the garments of the Spider. The wig of the Spider was on his head, the telltale cape about his shoulders. His face was still that of Blinky McQuade, without the glasses, but there was no time to remedy that.

Driving more slowly as he neared the scene of the robbery, Wentworth studied the streets. Twice in the shadows, he spotted police cars, heard the hum of their restless engines ready for pursuit. He spotted also a trash-removal truck with many men sheltered behind its steel sides. That truck would make a deadly ambuscade with which to block the street.

Wentworth wondered if all avenues of escape were blocked equally well. Once inside this cordon of police, it would be almost impossible to smash a way out—even for the Spider!

114

Yet Wentworth pushed on, his mind intent on the Red Hand's plan. The escape car was to have been parked here for several hours. The getaway driver, at zero hour, would maneuver the car free and cross to the space before the office... As the memory of those detailed instructions crossed his mind, Wentworth saw a closed car pull out from the curb and coast over before the bus company door! Everything was moving according to schedule! GRIMLY, WENTWORTH bore down on the accelerator. He hurtled around the corner, and—wedged the escape car against the curb! The getaway driver swung about, white-faced. His hand whipped to a shoulder gun and, at the same moment, Wentworth saw three policemen converging on the car with machine and riot guns! The driver paid no attention to them at all. He swung to his right, and... Good God, his gun was pivoting toward the girl clearly revealed by the lights about the door, the lookout! She glimpsed the movement even as Wentworth did and tension leaped through her body. A startled cry rose in Wentworth's throat. The slovenliness was gone from the girl's posture and with a shock that almost paralyzed him, Wentworth recognized her. Nita! Why, God in heaven, *Nita*... the lookout for the Red Hand! But....

Wentworth chopped off his amazement. His gun leaped to his hand and, quicker than thought, he hammered lead through the windshield of his car, past the angle of the bus. Three shots he squeezed out in a quick deadly rhythm, and all three bullets sped true. The escape driver was sledged forward over his wheel, pinned there while forty-five caliber slugs blasted through his skull. Seconds later, the police opened fire. Had they assumed the shots came from the driver? Wentworth was in a direct line behind him, and… Wentworth flung sideways, twisting the door handle and spilling to the pavement on his back. The windshield came crashing down on the spot where he had sat. Lead ripped jagged holes through the steel of the body. No way of telling whether they were stray shots, or whether the police had deliberately fired on him.

Swiftly, the Spider rolled under his car, worked toward the side nearer Nita. He could see the lower half of her body, crouched against the wall by the entrance. Wentworth cupped his hands.

"Down, Nita!" he called softly. "Down flat on the pavement!"

Through a momentary lull in the firing, his voice carried clearly. He could not see Nita's face, but her head jerked toward the sound of his voice. At the same instant, guns went crazy inside the bus office. A machine gun began to hammer from the window and on the sidewalk a policeman cried out in a strained inhuman voice. More guns were speaking from the doorway now. Three men boiled out and down the short flight of steps. A riot gun bellowed and one of them was blown backward a yard, folded over as if a gargantuan fist had caught him in the wind. But a fist couldn't tear a man open like that.

The machine gun wielded by a second bandit swept in a short murderous arc, its flame throwing a ghastly illumination over the street. Then the two men were running side by side across the walk, headed straight for Wentworth's car! Deliberately, a cold smile twisting his lips, Wentworth lifted his automatic. It was at that same moment that Nita, recovering from her surprise, started toward him also. She staggered as she ran. Wentworth heard her call his name in a strained, thin voice. She was looking at him, not at the killers, and she blundered against the machine gunner.

The man struck out viciously with his left hand. Wentworth saw metal glint in his fist and snapped a desperate shot at the man's shoulder, trying to arrest that blow... Too late. The shot was a clean miss. Nita was hurled violently to the pavement, her body rolling limply, her arms flung helplessly wide. Wentworth's guns were speaking again, throwing hard, accurate lead. The machine gunner went back on his heels with a bullet-smashed breastbone, then spilled forward across the path of his companion. As the second man tripped, Wentworth threw his seventh shot, heard the man scream, and saw the bandit's hands beat the pavement convulsively. Wentworth scarcely looked at him. Nita lay half in the street, head lolling laxly back on the pavement with that ridiculous little hat smashed over her right ear. There was a dark tracery of blood across her white cheek!

FRANTICALLY, WENTWORTH started out from under the coupé. One gun was empty and he thrust it into its holster, dragged out another. No time now to load....

As if a machine-gun battery had opened simultaneous fire, the street went mad with gun fire; Wentworth felt the car above him jerk and quiver under the hammer of lead, heard the deeper roar of riot guns blasting. A grenade burst somewhere near the front of the jammed bus, and the concussion half-stunned Wentworth. In God's name, what was happening here? No matter. He must get to Nita.

Wentworth wormed his way out from under the car on his belly, reached Nita's side—and past his outstretched legs a truck crunched, missing him by inches. He twisted about—and his eyes strained wide, tightened again in fury. An armored truck had ground to a halt almost over him and Nita. From its gun ports, lead and flame spewed in a constant stream. His gaze flicked over the street. Blue-coated police were sprawled in the awkward poses of death all about him in the paths of the brilliant police searchlights. Up near the corner, one man with a machine gun still answered the fire of the armored car but, even as Wentworth looked, he was hammered into oblivion by a blast of lead.

A grim smile twisted Wentworth's lips. With swift hands, he reloaded his empty automatic, then threw an arm around Nita and dragged her closer to the side of the truck. Carefully he lifted his automatic and aimed at the chain drive of the rear wheel. Two shots smashed it in two. He bent down and fired at the drive on the opposite side. Then he dragged Nita under the armored car.

The engine of the car was racing, its exposed gears whirring futilely. In a few moments… Wentworth hefted his automatic and once more the cold smile played over his lips. He had time to examine Nita's wound. Thank God, it was only a glancing blow. The scalp was torn above the temple, but it wasn't serious… His head jerked up. Inside the truck, he could hear men shouting. Abruptly, doors whanged open. From both sides and the rear men spilled out and landed running!

Instantly, from a car down the street, a police machine gun

opened again. Three men were fleeing across the open area of the street itself; four others had chosen the other side. Wentworth left the three to the police gunner and began a deliberate firing… Presently he holstered hot automatics and scrambled out from under the truck. Now was his chance, while police defenses were scattered. He could not delay with Nita wounded. Thank God, he had ordered Ram Singh to meet him here! The rendezvous was only two blocks away. Wentworth paused a moment, crouching before he lifted Nita into his arms. From his vest pocket, he slipped the thin platinum cigarette lighter which never left his person and with its base imprinted the seal of the Spider on the side of the truck.

Afterwards, he caught up Nita in his arms and ran, bent double, for the corner nearby, using the stalled bus for cover. There were shouts behind him. A bullet whined high, then he was around the corner. Three policemen lay in a welter where the machine guns of the armored truck had caught them, and Wentworth's face was white as he raced on. The police had won a victory, but it had cost them terribly to defeat the Red Hand!

The shouts of pursuers were louder. Only the fact that he used the route the armored car had followed saved him for the moment. As soon as police sighted him… Grimly, Wentworth recognized that they would cut him down without mercy. They only knew that he was running from the scene of the crime, carrying away the woman who had served as lookout!

A half breath ahead of police bullets, Wentworth whirled a corner. Another block to go to where Ram Singh had been ordered to await him. If Ram Singh were not there… Ah, good!

Ram Singh had spotted them. The Daimler backed into the street, spurted to meet him with its engine revving in reverse. A half dozen more strides....

Back on that death-strewn street, a siren ripped out. At the corner which Wentworth had just turned, a policeman's revolver opened up. Wentworth's chest labored for breath. Nita's weight in his arms seemed unbearable and the Daimler merely crawled. As it lurched to a halt beside Wentworth, the rear door flew open and behind its screen, he sprang to the running board with Nita. Instantly, the car was rolling forward again.

Braced against the lurching of the machine, Wentworth knelt to lay Nita tenderly upon the rear seat. Other sirens were shrieking on their trail. The Daimler's speed mounted like a diving plane. On a straightaway, it could leave the police hopelessly behind, but Ram Singh must do more than that. He must completely baffle pursuit... Well, he could do that with a few minutes' start. Wentworth must furnish that. He bent for a moment above Nita and it seemed to him that, even unconscious as she was, her lips answered his. He laughed, feeling his heart lift. The police had suffered terribly, yes, but a heavy blow had been struck at the Red Hand. His raiders would be shaken....

"Stop around the next corner," Wentworth called to Ram Singh. "I'll stop the police. You take the *missie sahib* home, regardless of what she says when she comes to. Her wound is slight."

Ram Singh's shoulders looked stubborn. "But, *sahib*," the Sikh's voice was harsh. "Let thy servant stop the police! Thou, master, can drive the *missie sahib*...."

"Silence!" Wentworth's voice became harsh, too. "It is a command!"

IT WAS three-quarters of an hour later, while Ram Singh still doubled through devious by-ways, that Nita van Sloan came to her senses in the rear of the car. There was a furious pain in her head, but her first conscious sensation was one of relief, or happiness; her memory was of Wentworth's voice, calling to her....

Ram Singh took the 86th Street crosscut under Central Park, rolled the Daimler smoothly to the curb before Wentworth's apartment—and four uniformed policemen rushed the car, whirled Ram Singh from his seat! Commissioner Kirkpatrick's tall, striding figure advanced briskly from the building. The entire thing had taken Nita completely by surprise, but she concealed an automatic against her thigh and waited.

Kirkpatrick's face was drawn and harsh as he opened the door. "You're under arrest, Nita," he said shortly.

Nita smiled. "I rather—guessed that much, Stanley—I believe it's customary to read a warrant or something."

Kirkpatrick said stonily, "The charge is murder in the first degree. You shot a policeman at the Central Bus robbery, but it was careless of you to leave a gun, registered in your name, on the scene."

Nita leaned forward sharply. "You're mad, Stanley," she cried.

"I'm afraid there's no mistake, Nita," Kirkpatrick said steadily. "I had ballistics experts check before I came here. A bullet from your gun killed him. Hurry, Nita. We waste time!"

Nita agreed quietly. The front door of the car stood open

where Ram Singh had been jerked from behind the wheel. The motor was still running. Careless of them.

"Yes, I suppose we do waste time," Nita said quietly. She stepped on the running board, jammed the muzzle of her automatic into Kirkpatrick's body!

"Don't anyone move," she cried, "or your commissioner dies!"

"You dare not shoot," Kirkpatrick said calmly.

"No?" Nita laughed harshly. "You came to arrest me for killing a policeman, remember. Stand right where you are, Stanley."

Nita backed into the front seat of the car, her gun still on Kirkpatrick, whipped the door suddenly shut as she jerked the car into gear. A police gun whanged, and the bulletproof glass starred beside her cheek. Nita winced, but her control of the car did not waver. She whirled the heavy Daimler around a corner.

Resolutely, Nita swung the nose of the Daimler toward the spot where Dick had stayed to block the pursuit. Behind her, sirens opened up. Her eyes narrowing, Nita flicked on the radio and tuned in police signals. Already, the police were weaving a net of radio cars across her path. Nita's teeth set on her lower lip to strangle down the wild laughter that rose. She felt small, helpless. It was not that she was afraid. She would not fear anything in the world with Dick beside her. But Dick... where was he?

CHAPTER 12
BLINKY McQUADE PAYS

A S SOON as Wentworth, waiting to block the pursuit of Nita, had sent a bullet home into the front tire of a police car, he took to his heels along the street. His few minutes of rest had revived him and, before the radio roadster had ceased its slithering skid across the street, he had reached the next corner.

As he ran along, he heard a bell toll distantly, chiming out the quarter hour. Quarter of one! So much had happened in that brief fifteen minutes; so many brave men had died! But the Red Hand had been scotched, and Nita was safe… Wentworth was almost cheered as he made his way rapidly eastward. He was due at Balmy's at one o'clock under orders from the Red Hand. It was two minutes after one o'clock when Blinky McQuade presented himself at the door.

"Is this a hell of a night!" he growled at the scar-faced Balmy. "Every corner you turn, there's another siren howling. And I heard shooting. Plenty of it. I hope the Red Hand's okay."

Balmy grunted as he padded behind the bar. "What kind of luck did you have?" he asked.

Wentworth looked at him for thirty seconds. "I'll take whisky," he said. "Beer chaser."

Balmy's gaze wavered as he set up bottle and glass. "Okay. Okay, you don't have to tell me, but I'm handing you orders from the Red Hand, same as I did these other guys."

Wentworth swung his head around, frowning over the spectacle. Three men were slouched down over their drinks. They looked disconsolate.

"Spill it," Wentworth ordered Balmy.

Balmy dug a square of white paper out of his pocket. Wentworth saw the hated signature of the Red Hand, then the paper was tossed on the bar. Wentworth bent close to read it:

"To all those who accepted the Red Hand's orders," it said. "You will place in the hands of Balmy eighty percent of your take. Payment must be by tomorrow noon. Fail us at your peril."

Wentworth took his time about it, with Blinky's blindness as an excuse. Something like elation sprang up within him. This gave him a further chance to fight the Red Hand. If he could persuade a few crooks to mutiny against this payoff, and guide them to safety, it would be a blow at the prestige of the Red Hand.

Wentworth granted. "Eighty percent, huh? That's damned high for a gander." He glowered at Balmy. "Well, it says noon, and noon is what it'll be. Go jump in the river, Balmy." He took the whisky bottle to the table where the three sat.

"I knew there was a catch in this Red Hand business," Wentworth said savagely. "Where the hell does he get off? Eighty percent! Look, you guys, let's get out of here anyway."

Balmy glared after them when they left and Blinky jeered at him. "Going where we can get some decent whisky, punk."

IT TOOK Wentworth almost an hour to talk the three men into mutiny, but in the end they all got in a car and headed out of New York through the Holland Tunnel. Wentworth drove with them as far as Rahway, then he insisted on separating. On the train back to New York, Wentworth worked on a project that brought a gleam to his eyes. Blinky McQuade was going to pay his eighty percent to the Red Hand, but he was going to have a record of the number of every bill he turned over—and every one would be marked! He thought that the Spider would be able to get police cooperation in tracing the bills stolen from the Grand Avenue Bus Company safe!

On the way back to his room, Blinky McQuade stopped by Balmy's and paid his tribute to the Red Hand, took Balmy's receipt for $17,080.00, eighty percent of the loot from the safe. Blinky McQuade moved wearily through the streets, but once inside his room, he sprang into swift action. The Spider still had work to do in the hour left before dawn. Before the makeup table hidden in the head of the bed, he built once more the harsh lines of the Spider's face; the lipless gash of the mouth and the cavernous eyes. Yes, there still was work to do! Clare Sutton and her father must talk; Bubbles Morval must tell where she got the dictation of the Red Hand. And then—perhaps there would be no need of the marked money!

Wentworth raced uptown to the Electra Building—and found the silken ropes that had bound Clare Sutton lying in fragments on the floor. He sped to Sutton's apartment, and found it empty except for a Chinese houseboy who jabbered quaveringly in Cantonese that Sutton *san* had not returned since the morning before.

Hard anger shone in Wentworth's eyes as he raced on the last leg of his night's investigation. Too late! But how could he have guessed that Sutton would take alarm? He shook his head. Nothing that he had done this night could have been put off for this piece of work—unless he had avoided that wild dash to the payroll robbery. Providence was guiding him there, the providence which Ram Singh called his *karma*, his and Nita's. A shudder swept over him. If he had not gone to the bus office, Nita would have been killed. Now, thank God, she was safe—safe for the rest of this battle with the Red Hand. He was winning....

Wentworth smiled thinly. He was claiming victory too soon. It was only that, since he had rescued Nita, his heart was so much lighter! A sudden thought struck him. Clare Sutton had escaped—and the Red Hand attack on the Central Bus Company offices had been almost overwhelming; three times as strong as the plans of the Red Hand had indicated. Only one interpretation to put on that. *Clare had warned the Red Hand!*

No use going on any further with this work, was there? It was only a question now of finding Sutton—and when he did... Doggedly, Wentworth hastened to the home of Bubbles Morval. She was the only direct means of contact he had with the Red Hand except for Big Johnny Gaynor. He thought that it would be simpler to make the girl talk. He went to Bubbles Morval's apartment, picked the lock of her door—and this place also was empty!

FROWNING, THE SPIDER stood in the middle of the girl's single room, staring at the cheap bits of bric-a-brac, the hand-made pillows and drapes with which she had attempted to furbish the place's second-rate shoddiness. Should he search this place? If he did it thoroughly, daylight would trap him here. A new thought struck him. Was it possible that the Red Hand was behind this series of disappearances? Seizing all those through whom the Spider might strike at him after the setbacks of the night?

Wentworth whirled to the door—stopped short at sight of an

opened envelope on a taboret. It was a message from the building's telephone operator.

"Mr. Ransome wants you to call him at once—no matter how late."

The false dawn was ghostly in the sky when Wentworth reached the apartment house in which Oscar Ransome had quarters. The hall attendant was asleep in his chair. Wentworth located Ransome's apartment number on the board and went up in the service elevator, which he operated himself. He could not make up his mind about Ransome's guilt. After he had seen Bubbles, he would know.

The kitchen entrance yielded to Wentworth's skill with a lock pick and he ghosted through into a large drawing room where gray light outlined furnishings dimly. As he made his way toward the sleeping quarters, a bell began to whir intermittently. A doorbell! The devil! Had someone spotted his entrance? Wentworth had just time to dodge behind a high-backed chair when he heard footsteps coming from the bedrooms—and, simultaneously, someone began to move in the servants' quarters. Wentworth hesitantly drew an automatic. The footsteps came rapidly nearer and—a girl ran into the drawing room, went swiftly toward the kitchen.

"Don't bother, Reed," she called. "I'll answer it!"

Wentworth frowned. Bubbles Morval! No doubt about her voice, but what in the name of heaven was she doing here? The flutter of her diaphanous robes made her almost unearthly in the gray light as she sped to the front door. She flung it wide.

"Oh, Donald, Donald!" she cried. "Thank God you've come! I've been worrying about you so!"

The door drifted slowly back against the wall and Wentworth could see the two in the light of the hall, like figures on an illuminated stage. Don Blaine stood with his shoulders sagging, his head bowed.

"Oh, Lord!" he whispered, and the sibilance of it reached to Wentworth's ears. "Lord, Bubbles, *you...*" He swung blindly away.

Bubbles cried out and ran after him. His blindly swung arm hurled her backward. Her shoulders struck the jamb and she wavered there during the seconds that an elevator door slammed out there in the hall. The strength drained out of her body then. Bubbles slid to the floor, weeping.

Out of the kitchen, a man, bundled in a dressing gown, hurried to her, "Oh, Miss!" he cried. "You mustn't stay there like that. 'Tisn't healthy."

Bubbles looked up at him dazedly and he had to repeat the words before she let him help her to her feet.

"Shall I call the master, Miss Morval?" Reed asked swiftly. "He left word I was to phone him at the club at the slightest need."

Bubbles shook her head wearily, dismissed Reed and crossed to sink into the very chair behind which Wentworth crouched. **HE WAITED** until sound ceased in the servant's quarters, until Bubbles began to sob softly, then he stepped forward.

"Keep quiet, Bubbles," he ordered crisply.

The girl's sobs ceased, then she sighed. "You... You heard

everything. He didn't give me a chance to explain. Mr. Ransome said he had been threatened again over the Taug evidence and he was afraid for me to stay at my place alone. And now, Donald...."

Wentworth leaned over her, rested a hand gently on her head. "Don't worry," he said softly. "It will all straighten out... Bubbles, you must answer some questions. Those instructions that you gave out tonight for the Red Hand resulted in many people being killed. If the police knew...."

Under his touch, Bubbles Morval stiffened. "The police!" she cried in a muffled voice. "But... *you* know. And people who don't fear the police fear you!"

A coldness crept into Wentworth's voice, "That is why you must answer my questions. Who dictated those notes that you transcribed in Ransome's office and gave out at Balmy's? How did you know whom to give them to?"

A strong shudder swept over Bubbles. Afterward, she relaxed. "I'm glad you came," she said quietly. "I'm going to tell you everything I know, but it isn't much. The man who dictated those messages called me on the telephone; the Red Hand seal was mailed to me. He also mailed me money, but... Oh, Spider, I saw the Red Hand kill a man, that man Sharps from Balmy's, and he said if I didn't do what he said... he'd kill Donald that way! If you could have heard that man's agony!"

She was trembling again. Wentworth strangled his disappointment.

"Where was Sharps killed?"

"The basement of the building where the man they call Big Johnny has offices... Balmy pointed out the people I had to give messages. I don't even know why the Red Hand wanted to use me. I… I don't know anything."

"The voice over the wire," Wentworth said softly. "Could it have been… *Ransome's?*"

Bubbles Morval shook her head. "When I was taking dictation yesterday, he was in his office. I could see him there and he wasn't using the phone."

Unless there were some very involved trickery, her evidence absolved Ransome! Damn it, Wentworth had to locate Sutton at once!

"As soon as you open the office today," he ordered flatly. "I'm coming there in disguise. When the Red Hand calls again, you must signal to me and I'll trace the call. Promise me that, and I'll do what I can to straighten out Blaine. Fail me—*and Blaine dies!*"

Wentworth was forced to drape the Spider's cape inconspicuously over his arm when he left the building. The red sun had thrust above the building tops. Soon it would be clear daylight and the streets would fill with early workers. But the Spider had yet another task to perform… He must examine the basement under Big Johnny Gaynor's office to see if it were regularly used by the Red Hand!

THE BASEMENT was a disappointment and Wentworth hurried from there to Holian Alley and the room of Blinky McQuade. Swiftly he altered his disguise to that of McQuade, threw himself down to sleep. He allowed himself three hours, sprang up greatly refreshed. Today, surely, after last night's defeats, the Red Hand would be beaten! Wentworth went out almost gaily to eat, taking along materials for a change of disguise. He would phone Nita just to reassure her. He… A glimpse of the front pages on a newsstand stunned him!

Across the front page of each paper was spread a picture of three men, the three men whom Wentworth had persuaded to mutiny against the Red Hand and whom he had escorted far into the safety of New Jersey. Handcuffed together, the three men had been chained in the early morning hours to the lamp standard of one of the green lights in front of the police head-quarters in Centre Street!

"Fastened around their necks," said the cut-lines, "was the proof of their crimes. These three are charged with the atrocious murder of the girl usher at the Bal Masque Theater. Police say the evidence is complete."

A harsh curse rasped in Wentworth's throat. So had the Red Hand answered his feeble attempt at mutiny! As for the other crimes… Dazedly, Wentworth read the toll: Twelve robberies had succeeded, twelve of which he had never heard. Of the many he had attempted to prevent, more than half had been success-ful and twenty-two police had been killed or wounded by the robbers. Two bus garages had burned with a loss of hundreds of thousands of dollars! Three buses had caught fire on the streets and the doors had jammed, trapping passengers! And twelve had died in the double-decker's dive off the viaduct.

Great God in heaven! And he had thought the Red Hand beaten! It was quite plain that Bubbles and Balmy constituted only one chain in a series of systems for distributing criminal "jobs." Truly, the Red Hand had the city completely within the grasp of that cruel steel gauntlet!

Another phase of the Red Hand's activity sprang to mind and Wentworth turned quickly to the stock market lists. There, too, the butcher had been crowned with success. But Wentworth had one thing to be grateful for. Nita was safe!

It was as he crumpled the newspaper to hurl it away that a small item on the front page caught his attention and the hands with which he drew the paper close to his eyes again trembled violently. That item contained Nita's name… Slowly, incredulously, he read that she was wanted for the murder of a policeman, that she had escaped arrest by throwing a gun on Commissioner Kirkpatrick, had finally got away from the police by abandoning her car and fleeing into the tangled streets of the underworld.

Nita… safe? What a mockery! The Red Hand had won on every point! Wentworth stood on the corner in the bright sunlight of early morning and his fists knotted whitely at his sides. It was the worn face of Blinky McQuade that lifted to the heavens, but it was the soul of the Spider which swore the oath—Today, *today*, the Red Hand must die!

CHAPTER 13
THE SPIDER STRIKES

WENTWORTH FORCED himself to delay long enough for food, then he made his way swiftly to the employment agency of Big Johnny Gaynor. Less than twenty-four hours ago, Blinky McQuade had come here to enlist in the army of the Red Hand. He should have destroyed Gaynor then! He knew that now, but he had hoped to learn more by allowing the agency to operate.

Once more the office was jammed with criminals. Wentworth knew the type, but the faces were entirely unfamiliar. Was the Red Hand importing killers then? Coldly, Wentworth determined that Big Johnny should talk before he died!

Throughout the hour that Blinky McQuade was kept waiting he listened intently to the voices around him, but apparently these men knew only that they were needed by the Red Hand—and were driven by greed and fear to serve him! His cohorts had served the Red Hand well last night! One more such night of terror, and anarchy would rule the city! The police, even forewarned, had been all but powerless against the superb organization of the Red Hand.

When finally, Wentworth was admitted to Gaynor's private office, he had to force himself to walk slowly. He wanted to charge into that sanctum with his guns ready. But Gaynor was only a cog in the Red Hand's machine. So Wentworth cautioned himself—and he advanced with the shambling, groping gait of Blinky McQuade. Gaynor was tipped back as usual, feet on the desk, big unlighted cigar dwarfing his grimacing face.

"Well, Blinky," he grinned. "You pulled it off last night, eh? Come back for another job, eh?"

Blinky McQuade peered, frowning above his spectacles. "I pulled it off, yeah. Listen, I got some dope for the Red Hand."

Gaynor took the cigar out of his mouth and yawned, but Wentworth could see how keenly the small black eyes quested over his face. "Okay," said Gaynor. "Spill it."

"To you, punk? Listen, this goes to the Red Hand himself or nobody. It's important." Wentworth saw scorn on Gaynor's face. "Wait, Gaynor, listen. I know how to find the Spider!"

Gaynor whipped his feet off the desk. "Spill it!" he ordered in a hard voice, and jumped up, still a head shorter than Blinky McQuade.

"You talk," Gaynor said, "or I'll by God have it squeezed out of you! There's a basement here where you can make all the noise you like—and nobody hears. And I got the men. Talk and talk fast!"

"Okay, okay," Wentworth put McQuade's whine into his voice. "But listen, I got to get credit, see." He dropped his voice, leaned over the desk toward Gaynor. "Listen, the Spider has got a place…."

His hands moved with abrupt speed and closed around Gaynor's throat. He dragged the smaller man across the desk, threw him flat on the floor. With a cold impersonality, he squeezed until Gaynor's eyes were popping, until his face was dark red with congested blood. Then he relaxed his hold a little….

"Ready to talk, Gaynor?" he said softly. "Ready to talk… *to the Spider!*"

GAYNOR WAS breathing hoarsely. His head rolled. Wentworth drew out his cigarette lighter and pressed the base on Gaynor's hand.

"Well, Gaynor?"

Gaynor lifted his hand slowly, then his mouth stretched in a scream that Wentworth's quick grip just choked. "The Spider!" Gaynor's lips formed the words soundlessly, "The Spider!"

"Now, talk, Gaynor," Wentworth ordered coldly, "or by heavens that seal will go on your forehead!"

Gaynor jerked his head in assent and Wentworth eased his hold. "I don't know where the Red Hand is," Gaynor whispered huskily. "I got to call somewhere and then he calls me. And they got to hear my voice. They know it. Honest to God, Spider, I don't know who he is or where he is. He always wears that damned mask. I...."

Gaynor sprang backward and his hand whipped under his coat to a gun. Easy for Wentworth to beat him to the draw, to blow him down, but the noise would bring killers pouring in here. With a prodigious bound, Wentworth whipped his right fist to Gaynor's jaw. It was a tremendous blow. Gaynor was lifted off his feet, hurled backward head-first... straight at the steam radiator! Wentworth tried to catch him, but it was impossible. Gaynor's head struck with a violence that made the pipes ring. His body bent at the waist, knees whipping up toward his face, then he collapsed in a heap.

Wentworth caught his balance, a fierce oath in his throat, crouched by the man to feel for the pulse. Dead! Stone dead. If anyone should come to investigate that noise... He caught up Gaynor and thrust him into a chair against the front wall, stood by the door. A moment later he heard it open behind him.

"That's the way it is, Gaynor," Wentworth whined. "Hell, a guy can't make a living on twenty percent of his take..." His voice changed abruptly, became the rasping twang of Gaynor.

"You want me to tell the Red Hand that?" he said, with menace in his tones. "Get away from that door, you!"

The door closed sharply and Wentworth sprang to the secret recess in the desk top. Rapidly, he ran through the sheets of the Red Hand's "jobs." As he read he felt his heart begin to throb with long, hard pulses. Nothing here to show what would be attacked, but on twenty different jobs, the Red Hand called for men experienced in setting fires that would spread with instantaneous killing heat! In eight others, he called for dynamiters! The Spider needed no more than this to tell him the Red Hand was bent on a murder march that would pale last night's massacres into insignificance! But where and when would he strike? He had to find the Red Hand and kill him. He *had* to....

Meantime, here in one room were some of the men who would do these jobs for the Red Hand. In one room! Slowly, Wentworth began to smile. He caught up the telephone and called police headquarters.

"The Spider speaking, Kirkpatrick," he said flatly. "Tonight, the Red Hand is planning crimes that will make last night seem a pleasant holiday. If I can, I will get you details later. Meantime... in Big Johnny Gaynor's office, you will find some hundred men who will work tonight for the Red Hand, unless you round them up. On suspicion charges, we'll say. Good, Kirkpatrick! Sometimes, you think fast! I'll try to hold them until you get here. And, incidentally, Kirkpatrick, I was forced to kill Gaynor. Oh, purely self-defense, I assure you!"

He hung up the phone, polished it clean of prints. It would take Kirkpatrick five minutes to assemble a force of men adequate to the job; another ten minutes to get here and surround the building. In fifteen minutes, then, he must be gone, but meantime there must be no suspicion that Gaynor was dead. He began talking, first in Blinky's voice, then in Gaynor's, while he sought some further clue to the Red Hand or his whereabouts. There was nothing. Gaynor kept his office clean in event of a raid; clean except for these hidden "job" lists of the Red Hand.

Wentworth crossed to the window and knotted a length of the Spider's silken "web" to the radiator and let it dangle into space. That should show how the Spider escaped and clear Blinky McQuade of any suspicion. When ten of the fifteen minutes he had allowed the police were elapsed, Wentworth walked out of the office.

"So long, Johnny," he grumbled as he left. He stopped by the man who watched the door. "Johnny says he don't want nobody in there for ten minutes. He's got to call the boss."

"Sure, Blinky," the man agreed. "You tell him something to tell the boss?"

Wentworth told him roughly to mind his own business, and thus confirmed the man's belief. Then he groped his way to the street. As he rounded a corner in retreat, three carloads of police emptied on the side street near Gaynor's office. But Wentworth was frowning as he hurried toward Ransome's office. The Red Hand had more than one link with the underworld. And tonight... there would be twenty fires; eight dynamitings.

Unless the Spider acted.

WENTWORTH EFFECTED swift changes in makeup in the washroom of a subway station and emerged square-shouldered and striding, a dapper black mustache on his upper lip, the infirmities of Blinky McQuade and his peering glasses discarded. As always with his disguises, it was as much the mannerisms he adopted as the facial distortion which changed his appearance. He had purchased a bright blue shirt and canary yellow tie. He tapped his hat brim jauntily to Bubbles Morval as he entered Ransome's office.

"How're you, beautiful?" he grinned. "Where's the boss?"

Bubbles Morval looked him over disdainfully. "Out," she said, and turned back to her typing. Wentworth leaned closer, and his voice became the flat tone of the Spider.

"I told you I'd come in disguise," he said softly. "Do you know where Ransome is?"

Bubbles Morval whirled toward him, face drawn. "You!" she whispered. "You are… the…."

"Never mind," Wentworth cautioned sharply. "What about Ransome?"

Bubbles shook her head. "I haven't seen him or heard from him," she said. "I don't know what to make of it. He had an important case coming up this morning. I managed to get an adjournment, but I'm worried…."

"No word from the Red Hand? Or from Blaine?"

Bubbles Morval shook her head again, eyes clouding at mention of Don Blaine. There was nothing for it except to wait. Wentworth made one telephone call, to the telephone company offices, and gave quick, concise instructions. He was very confident that Bubbles would receive a call today from the Red Hand. According to his deductions, the Red Hand knew that the Spider had learned his plans from Bubbles' notes. The Red Hand was too shrewd not to use that fact to trap the Spider.

It was four o'clock in the afternoon when Bubbles Morval, taking up the phone, signaled Wentworth that it was the Red Hand who called!

"Just a minute," Bubbles said, "till I get my notebook. Oh, sir, you promised me nothing would happen to Donald, and... All right. All right, I'm ready."

Before she had begun to take dictation, Wentworth was in touch by another line with the telephone company. They were instantly busy, tracing the call. He heard Bubbles' voice in the other room, constantly delaying the dictation. The Red Hand would be certain to grow suspicious. Wentworth smiled thinly as he waited. He thought the Red Hand would make sure the message came through, for by it, he would hope to trap the Spider!

"On the call to Mr. Ransome's office," the telephone official's dry voice spoke, "we have succeeded in tracing the call and it is coming from Mr. Ransome's home."

Wentworth started swiftly toward the outer office, checked as he heard the main door open. Two uniformed men, led by two plainclothes police, came striding in.

"You Bubbles Morval?" one of the detectives demanded.

Bubbles took the time to hang up, to close her book and slide it into an open drawer. "I'll have to know your business before I answer that," she said quietly.

"You don't have to," the cop told her. "Take her, Bill. Ransome here?"

Bubbles Morval was on her feet. "No, he isn't," she said sharply. "You'll have to show your authority before you can search this office!" She moved to intercept the detective, but he thrust her back into the seat, came striding toward where Wentworth crouched behind the door. He peered in, saw the room apparently empty.

"Look in that other office, Frank," he ordered. "And you, Miss, you're under arrest for possessing stolen property. You paid your rent today with money that was stolen from the Grand Avenue Bus Company last night. Ransome is wanted for murder. He bumped off a broker down in Wall Street this morning. Listen, Morval, we know your boss is the Red Hand, and it may go easier with you if you spill what you know. Not in there either, Frank? Pick up this dame's notebook. She was writing in it, something over the phone."

Wentworth's movement was silent. He ground his gun muzzle into the big cop's spine, leveled another on the three other men.

"Lift them straight up," he ordered quietly.

THOSE POLICE knew the accent of command. Their hands flew up.

"Get their guns, Bubbles," Wentworth ordered, "and put their handcuffs on them. That's right, cross them up. Now, your notebook."

Three minutes later, they were walking quietly along the corridors. Behind them, the cops were shouting, but it would be minutes before they could get anyone to them, many more minutes before they got free, since Wentworth had the handcuff keys. He took Bubbles to the floor above and the elevator dropped them swiftly. As they entered a taxi, Wentworth told her about tracing the call to its source.

Bubbles gasped. "But that isn't possible! It isn't Mr. Ransome. I know it isn't!"

"It doesn't have to be," Wentworth agreed quietly. "That money you paid out for rent. Where did you get it?"

"It was in my mailbox this morning when I went by home," she told him immediately. "My pay from the Red Hand!"

So the marked money had reached its goal! Wentworth made Bubbles leave the taxi as they sped through the hotel district.

"Buy luggage and clothing," he told her. "Don't use the Red Hand's money *unless* you must. Go to a hotel and register under an assumed name. When it's safe for you to reappear I'll put an ad in the *Times* personals."

He took her notebook and sped on toward Ransome's apartment. That phone call was in line with the other attempts to throw suspicion on Ransome, but he would have to hurry. Police bent on Ransome's arrest would certainly take over his home soon....

Once more, he went over the message which the Red Hand had given to Bubbles Morval—for delivery to Blinky McQuade! The fact that the message was addressed to him might mean that McQuade was suspected! That was unimportant if it allowed Wentworth to reach the Red Hand. The message read:

The Red Hand needs you on a job which he will lead personally, the looting of a collection car of the B.M.R. subway. There

is a safe to be opened. Be at southbound platform Bowling Green station at 6:15 p.m. Get on train that flies red flag. Fail us at your peril.

Wentworth smiled faintly. If he had needed proof that this was a trap, he received the guarantee in that phrase "The Red Hand... will lead personally." Collection car of a subway. Last night, the Red Hand had attacked the buses. Tonight—the *subways and the elevated trains!* And the Red Hand had called for arson experts and dynamiters.

FURIOUSLY, WENTWORTH flung from the taxi as it reached Ransome's address. He duplicated his picking of the service entrance lock, ran soft-footed through the suite with gun in hand. Whoever had called from here must be gone now, and at any moment the police might come. The phone was in Ransome's den. At the door, Wentworth paused, his habit of caution asserting itself. The Red Hand had expected this call to be traced, else he would not have used Ransome's phone.

Wentworth turned the knob, sprang aside as he whipped open the door. Even so, he was stunned by the hot blast of lead-torn air that whipped past his ear. The opening of the door had discharged a double-barreled shotgun, aimed to strike in the body any who entered that door! Wentworth stared at the device with nausea gnawing at his stomach, then he whirled and fled. The trap was proof enough that the Red Hand was no longer here, and the police....

He was on the pavement a half block away when the police cars began to slam to the curb before the house. He saw Kirkpatrick's tall striding figure cross the walk... Kirkpatrick must be warned what threatened tonight. There was one more obstacle they would throw in the path of the Red Hand. Balmy's Bit House and China Sam's, used for distributing the messages of the Red Hand, could be cleaned out, the occupants arrested. And suppose the police instead of Blinky McQuade, should await that collection car tonight!

Wentworth shook his head. There was no guarantee that the Red Hand would be aboard. That statement was merely bait for the trap. What was sure was that the Spider, if captured, would be taken to the Red Hand. That made his own course clear. The Spider must keep the appointment and allow himself to be captured, the Spider—*and Blinky McQuade!* Otherwise, he would confess that the Spider and McQuade were one and the same man! The identity must be preserved, for he could not be sure that tonight would end the battle. The Spider—and Blinky McQuade… But first Kirkpatrick must be warned, must be told to raid China Sam's and Balmy's; and to prohibit all trading in subway stocks if possible. That would curtail the Red Hand's profits!

From a drug store, Wentworth phoned Ransome's home, got Kirkpatrick on the wire and told of the impending attacks on subway and elevated; told him also that the Red Hand had laid a trap for the Spider and that he intended to enter it.

"Alone?" Kirkpatrick asked shortly. "You can't do that."

"Why not? Too dangerous?" Wentworth laughed.

"Too dangerous, yes, *for the city!* You have no right to risk the city's welfare that way. If you fail, the clue dies with you. Let me go with you!"

For a moment, Wentworth did not answer, then he laughed softly. The Spider—*and Blinky McQuade!* Why not? It would be good to have Kirkpatrick's steady strength beside him in the crisis.

"What," he said mockingly, "you fight side by side with the Spider?"

Kirkpatrick replied quietly, "I have fought side by side with Dick Wentworth."

It was an answer and a challenge.

"I'll give you my word," Kirkpatrick raced on, "that until the Red Hand is dead, I will make no attempt to arrest you."

"But afterward...."

"Afterward, I am the Commissioner of Police!"

Wentworth laughed harshly. Side by side into peril, into the trap of the Red Hand. He would go gladly, happily, if only he could know that Nita was safe!

To Kirkpatrick, he said flatly, "It's a deal!"

CHAPTER 14
INTO THE TRAP!

THE CAR in which Nita fled was hit a score of times by police bullets before she gained enough on the pursuit to stop and dodge into the doorway of a tenement. The tenements were never locked and their backyards and roofs furnished continuous avenues of escape, which police could close only by blockading the entire block. Nita gave them no time for that.

Directly across a back court, through another hallway and out again on a dark side street; repeat the performance....

It was an hour later that Nita once more reached the under-world haunts where she had crossed the trail of the Red Hand. It was the Red Hand, undoubtedly, that she had to thank for the murder frame. The means by which he had identified her was plain. She had been so foolish to carry a gun registered in her own name! She carried one of Dick's heavy forty-fives now—and it was inconspicuous.

Nita had been busy during the last hour. Purchases made skillfully at a half dozen spots had given her the materials, and now her lovely hair was straight and streaked with gray, her clothing was nondescript cast-offs and its bagginess, the black shawl across her shoulders effectually concealed her trim figure. So the gun was not conspicuous in the loose sack of the blouse. Confident in this disguise, she entered a cheap bar room where no one gave her a second glance as she crouched over successive glasses of beer. It was the last place police would seek a girl like Nita—and she could keep her ears open. It was after five o'clock in the morning when sight of a man staggering into the saloon pulled Nita abruptly erect in her seat. He slopped up against the bar, drank two quick whiskies and slapped money on the mahogany. Nita had seen the man only once at a distance, but she was sure of his identity. She paid her own score and when the man reeled out, she stopped him.

"Ain't your name Blaine?" she mumbled.

The man swayed on rubbery legs. "Don Blaine," he said thickly. "'S me. What about it?"

"Used to know a buddy of yours. Sergeant Blum," Nita told Blaine. "Come on, I'll buy a drink."

"Don't know Blum," Blaine said, then he giggled. "But I'll take that drink. Take a lot of drinks. Gonna drink myself to death."

Nita guided him into a booth in another barroom. "Sounds silly," she offered.

"Not silly," Blaine assured her. "Girl I'm in love with spent the night with her boss. Me, had a chance to spend night with *my* boss. Turned it down. Just like that." He made a sweeping motion of his hand that turned over his glass. He didn't notice it. "Going to marry my boss if I don't drink myself to death first."

"You got a woman boss, I guess," Nita put in.

"'S right!" Blaine nodded profoundly. "You're smart. Gotta woman boss. *Lady* boss. We're going to be married, but... we gotta wait."

"Wait for what, Don?"

Blaine winked. "Till this Red Hand gets caught."

Nita bent sharply forward. "What do you mean, you can't get married till the Red Hand gets caught?"

Blaine winked again. "Fact. But don't you try to get me to talk. I'm off women. Offa them. My girl spending the night... the night..." Blaine hiccoughed softly and his face screwed up. He said in a suddenly normal voice. "You see it's Bubbles I really love." He stared at Nita owlishly and after a while he blinked and tears slid down his cheeks. "She's a little tramp, but she's the one I really love."

IT WAS broad day before Nita got him out of the bar and took

him to the address he gave her. He
fell across the bed and Nita dropped
into a chair. Was there some meaning hidden in what he had said? She
doubted it. Her brain would not work.
She tried to read the morning paper
she had bought, but once she ascer-
tained it said nothing about Dick's

being captured, she lost interest... She could not tell what awak-
ened her, but she was sitting bolt upright with her eyes wide
open and the late afternoon sun slanted across the floor. Blaine
still slept heavily across the bed, and the door was shut, but...
Nita jerked to her feet. An envelope lay just inside the door. She
snatched it up.

"Dear Don," the note began, "At 6:15 p.m. today the Red
Hand will be aboard a collection car of the B.M.R. subway
which will stop at that time at the downtown platform of the
Bowling Green station. I'm going to try to hold him until police
come or something. If you captured him, you might get back
on the force. Don't think I'm making up to you. I don't care if I
never see you again. You should have more faith in me. Bubbles."

A slight smile moved Nita's lips. She decided that she
approved of Bubbles. But this was vital information. She must
get to Dick with it, and... She stopped in despair. She had no
idea at all where Dick was or what disguise he was wearing!

"Who in the hell are you?" a man's voice asked calmly.

Nita spun about, forgetting for the moment the age her
disguise indicated. Blaine was sitting up; gripping his head,

147

but staring at her with narrowed eyes. Nita swiftly made up her mind.

"Nita van Sloan," she told him coolly, in her normal voice. "I found you drunk last night and tried to pump you to see if I could learn something about Richard Wentworth, whom you helped to frame."

A slight grin touched Blaine's lips. "You've got a nerve, admitting it," he said thickly. He pushed groaning to his feet.

"A letter for you," Nita held out the message from Bubbles.

Blaine grunted, "You've got a nerve," he repeated, "but I don't know that I like it. Opening somebody else's letter is a penal offense!"

Nita smiled. "It didn't come by mail."

Blaine read the note swiftly and blood mounted to his cheeks, then he shrugged. "I guess you knew all about Bubbles anyway, if I can judge by the size of my head this morning." He read the thing over again, uttered an exclamation and caught his watch from his pocket. "Six-fifteen," he said. "I got twenty minutes."

Nita said quietly, *"We've* got twenty minutes. It's too late to… look for help." She meant to look for Dick. Her hand went to the bulge of the heavy gun in her blouse. "Bubbles sounds like a fine girl."

Blaine was jerking open a drawer, grabbing cartridges. "Too fine for me, I guess," he said harshly. "Listen, I'm going alone."

Nita smiled a little, her lips tight. The forty-five was ridiculously large against the slim whiteness of her hand. But she held it competently.

Blaine said savagely, "All right. There isn't time to argue. Come on!"

THEY RAN a half block and found a taxi. This was too simple, too easy, Nita told herself. If Bubbles Morval was not in league with the Red Hand, how had she learned this fact? And yet the Red Hand had treated her as a prisoner that night when they had been captured together.

She said it aloud. "This is too easy."

Blaine's head jerked toward her. "Miss van Sloan," he said, brokenly, "how did Bubbles find this out? She couldn't be in with those crooks. She couldn't be! I got taken prisoner by them last night. They kept me for hours tied up in a basement and then just turned me loose. And one of the guys that did it said... said a woman had been to see the boss. You see... One reason I got drunk last night. I went to Ransome's trying to find out something about Bubbles because she wasn't at home. And Bubbles was there. God, did that man mean Bubbles went to 'the boss' *that way?*"

"She told you to have faith," Nita said quietly. "But listen, Mr. Blaine. This is too easy. I think there's some trap. Either Bubbles didn't write that note...."

"She did!"

"Then Bubbles has been fooled, too," Nita went on. "At the subway, we'll separate. Keep in with the crowd until you can see a chance to do something. If you see the Red Hand...."

Blaine looked at her without words and Nita smiled with tight lips. "I shall shoot to kill!" she said.

The subway platform was crowded with home-bound people.

Nita's eyes quested over the weaving throng, and rested finally on the shambling figure of a man who stood near the lower end of the platform. His hair was sprinkled with gray and he wore curious spectacles, each lens shaded by a green hood. Something strangely familiar about that man, but it was not Dick. She would know Dick anywhere, in any disguise. Nevertheless, she moved toward the spot. Of Bubbles Morval, there was no trace. Nita glanced at the clock. Twelve minutes after six.

Then abruptly, she saw Bubbles. The girl was half behind one of the supporting pillars and her face was utterly pale. Her eyes, too, were fixed on the stooped man with the curious glasses. Nita's heart tightened with a sudden thought. Was it possible that… that the stooped man was… *the Red Hand?*

At the thought, Nita's hand brushed once more the heavy automatic she carried. But she would have to be *sure!* She shut her eyes, trying to remember the carriage of the man who had worn the mask of the Red Hand… It did not help. Her eyes flicked to the clock. *Six-fifteen!* A collection car, Bubbles had said. Even as the thought crossed Nita's mind, a double-car train slid into the station. There was a red flag fluttering at its forward end. Nita saw Bubbles start forward, saw tension creep into Blaine's body. With sudden determination, Nita began to fight her way through the crowd. A single door at the forward end of the train opened and the queer, stooped man with the hooded spectacles groped his way forward.

He paused an instant in the very door and then, from the shadows, sprang a figure that brought an involuntary cry to Nita's lips, a hunched figure in a black cape that flapped behind him with the speed of his leap, a man with a black hat drawn low over his forehead. *The Spider!* Only an instant was he visible, then his hands struck the spectacled man on the shoulders, hurled him inside and sprang in after him. Blaine was leaping across the temporarily bare spot on the platform. Nita heard Bubbles scream and her mind swung suddenly into swift, incisive alignment. She knew what she must do and why. Blaine made the door and it snapped shut. Instantly, the train began to slide out of the station… A despairing cry leapt to Nita's lips. Despite the closed doors, she ran after the rapidly accelerating train.

"Dick!" she sobbed. "Oh, Dick…."

INSIDE THE collection car, everything was darkness. Tunnel lights could not penetrate the windows and the illumination that crept in through the temporarily open door was feeble. That was the one factor on which Wentworth had not counted. Everything else had moved perfectly on schedule. Kirkpatrick, in the guise of Blinky McQuade, had blocked the air-operated door so that it could not close and that in turn, through various automatic safety devices, had kept the train from moving. So there had been no chance that it would pull out before both men were aboard.

The Spider's plunging leap from the shadows thunderbolted both himself and Kirkpatrick through the door, but Wentworth could not see to fall clear. Instead of coming up, guns in hand, on opposite sides of the car as they had planned, The Spider and Kirkpatrick sprawled together to the floor. In the instant they struck, another man fell violently across Wentworth's back. The train was immediately in motion. The closing of the door

151

completed the blackness. The motors hummed with powerful acceleration.

Despite the upset in plans, Wentworth's lightning-swift reflexes sprang to his aid. As the man fell across his shoulders, Wentworth whipped both hands upward and back, found the man's head. His hands locked on the back of the man's neck, Wentworth twisted and rolled to the floor. If he had been standing upright, he would have thrown his assailant a dozen feet. As it was, the wrench hurled him clear. Wentworth came softly erect, back against the wall, automatics in hand. He crouched there, listening, waiting. All about him was the deepening thunder of the train diving for the swoop under the broad reaches of the lower East River. Almost imperceptibly, speed began to slacken. But nothing else happened. There was no further attack, no sound from the man he had thrown. And no light.

With sudden determination, Wentworth whipped out a flashlight and threw its beam straight upward at the ceiling. Without spotlighting either himself or Kirkpatrick, he spread a glow over the entire car. Kirkpatrick was crouched against the other wall with guns in hand. On the floor lay the unconscious form of—Wentworth repressed a start—of Don Blaine! And that was all. Except for themselves, the car was empty!

Slowly, the Spider sent the light questing forward and back. They were in the center portion of the first car of a two-car train. At either end of the car, a steel partition, in which gun slots had been cut, shut them in. They were neatly trapped. Whenever the Red Hand wished, he could turn on the lights and, through those gun-slots, fill their bodies with lead! Yet the only change since their entrance was the gradually diminishing speed. The train was barely crawling now, the motors not pulling at all; occasionally air hissed into the brakes.

Wentworth holstered a gun, crossed to examine Blaine. "Not badly hurt, thank God," he said to Kirkpatrick. "I didn't know who he was."

Kirkpatrick straightened away from the wall. "A neat trap," he said. "Not a chance of getting out. They can kill us without exposing themselves. No telling what horror the Red Hand is planning, but we've had a sample."

Wentworth's lips grew grim. There had been samples all right. Arson and dynamite. An explosion had dumped the roof in on a speeding City Subway train and trapped hundreds under tons of debris. Twenty dead already had been taken out when he and Kirkpatrick had hurried to this rendezvous; and the Red Hand seemed to have scattered horror along their route. No more than a half mile from this trap, the sedan in which they had sped southward had been bathed in fire; fire that streaked down on their limousine from above!

Instantly, they had halted, jumped from the car—and beheld upon the elevated structure, an entire string of cars wrapped in flame! The Red Hand's arson experts knew their trade! Kirkpatrick and the Spider had labored side by side to rescue a few from the inferno that the train of wooden cars had instantly become. The fire department had taken over the hopeless battle within a few minutes, and the Spider had sped on, more grimly determined than ever to enter the Red Hand's trap—and turn it against that murdering ruler of hell! Now, they had entered the trap—and they were helpless!

"Greetings, Spider," a cool voice spoke, seemingly at Wentworth's elbow. He whirled, his guns licking upward—and there was nothing there. He saw then that the voice came through a grating in the steel blockade. He extinguished his light. Instantly, four other lights sprang into life, thrust through apertures high in the partitions.

"I cannot allow you to remain in darkness like this," the voice went on. "Ah, you have knocked out Blaine. Too bad. I wanted him to hear what I am about to reveal. No doubt, Spider, you are wondering about your fate?"

Wentworth reached the bulkhead in a stride, crouched to peer through the grating, but steel shields made it impossible to shoot. The Red Hand chuckled.

"Give up, Spider," he said. "You're caught like—forgive the trite simile—like a rat in a trap. I use it advisedly.

No doubt you have drowned rats in one of those old fashioned wire traps? No? Well, at least you can imagine what it's like. Presently, there will be some help for your imagination.

"Doubtless, you have noticed that we are going very slowly? Trains are piling up behind us, trains full of home-bound people at intervals of about a hundred and fifty feet, all the way under the river. We shall stop entirely in a little while, at a point I have picked very carefully. A point at which this car will be neatly covered when... Are you beginning to get the idea, Spider?"

Wentworth understood, and a rage that burned his heart made him tremble with the desire to kill, to kill the beast who

154

could plan such a thing. *Like rats in a trap!* Yes, it was an apt simile for the hundreds and thousands on these trains. They would die just like that when the Red Hand dynamited the tube—*and let the river in!*

CHAPTER 15
WHEN THE RIVER CAME IN

FOR ONCE, Wentworth's stoic calm deserted him. Rage tempted him to hurl bodily against that barrier, to smash futile lead against the steel. He forced himself to thrust his guns away, stood very straight in the middle of the scarcely moving car. He regained mastery and, as always, his swift brain sought to make the most out of the situation. Except for the barrier, he was face to face with the Red Hand. He might be able to identify the voice tones; if he were clever, he might get the Red Hand to admit before Kirkpatrick that Nita and he had been framed for the murder charges. None of that would mean anything if they died in this trap, but it was not in Wentworth's nature to despair. He said, in his heart, "I am not yet dead!"

But when he spoke to the Red Hand, his voice sounded weary, completely resigned. "You've been too clever for all of us from the start. The few blows I struck at you today through the police haven't accomplished much."

The Red Hand laughed. "Not much. Inconvenienced me a trifle."

"Of course, you'll have to pick a new rendezvous," Wentworth continued, "and find somebody else to give out your

The subway tunnel was filling with water as the battered
refugees clambered along the sidewalk.

orders…" Wentworth sat down against the side wall. "May as well make yourself comfortable, Blinky, the Red Hand doesn't do things by halves. When he traps you, you stay trapped. Look how cleverly he framed Wentworth and Nita van Sloan."

"A cinch," the Red Hand put in from beyond the barrier. "In each case, I just got hold of a gun that could be identified, killed with it and left the gun for the police to find. Very simple indeed. Of course the set-up on Wentworth was a little more elaborate. By the way, I've framed Blaine there the same way. I trust the water will revive him"—his voice became vicious—"I want him to know what's happening…! The louse had the nerve to fall in love with my secretary!"

Wentworth saw Kirkpatrick's head swing quickly about, knew that he had caught the meaning behind the words. By saying Blaine had fallen in love with "my secretary," he was identifying himself as… *Oscar Ransome!* Wentworth's eyes narrowed, but he said nothing about the circumstance.

"Blinky!" The Red Hand's voice rang out. "Perhaps you wonder why I have doomed you with this other creature I hate?"

Kirkpatrick swung his head about, frowning as Wentworth had taught him, and Wentworth's heart contracted. Had the Red Hand penetrated the fact that Blinky and the Spider were one? If he had, despite his clever story to Kirkpatrick, the disguise was worthless in the future….

Kirkpatrick whined, "Geez, chief, I ain't done nothing!"

The Red Hand laughed jarringly, "You only encouraged three good men not to pay up my percentage of their take!" The voice came viciously through the panel. "It was clever of you to have someone else take the risk, to see if you could get away with it. But you mutinied against me, Blinky. That is enough."

Kirkpatrick did not trust himself to speak further in the strained accents of Blinky McQuade, and the Red Hand laughed again. "I leave you to your prayers. Your time won't be long now!"

Wentworth smiled across at Kirkpatrick. "Blinky McQuade is going to have a surprise tomorrow, if we don't get out of here. He'll read that he is dead. He'll be damned glad that I intercepted the message of the Red Hand to him, and tied him up in his room. I was planning to disguise myself like him tonight, but I think you make a much better Blinky."

Kirkpatrick said, in a muffled voice, "Damn your jesting. We've got to get out of here and stop this fiend!"

"We will," Wentworth said quietly.

HIS GLANCE was questing over the steel-lined chamber in which they sat. He saw now that the covering on windows and doors was steel; that the emergency door opening device, usually placed beside each door, was not included in this car's equipment. There were some air tubes overhead. What would happen if he punctured one with a bullet? Obviously, he would release the air in some circuit, and the doors he knew, were operated by the release of compressed air. Hope began to quicken his pulse. It was a chance, of course. But when should he strike? How long before the Red Hand—let the river in?

Wentworth dared not let himself think of those train loads of human beings behind him, going home after weary hours in the office; each bound for the haven which every man and woman builds for himself with four walls and the warmth of love. *Rats in the Red Hand's trap!* But he must strike now; must risk the shot at once, or it would be too late. Water would short-circuit the third rail, stall the trains. Their human cargo would be immured in the darkness. Death would be all about them, by drowning; by trampling in the instantaneous panic that the explosion would bring.

Abruptly, the train jarred to a halt! "You won't have so terribly long to wait now, Spider," the Red Hand jeered at him. "We're stopping to derail this train. Some other lads of mine are doing the same on the other side of the river. There won't be a chance, Spider, not a chance in the world."

The train lurched forward again, lunged sideways and ground to a halt. "There, that's done, Spider. Well, good evening! Remember me when the water is up to your chins. And remember, too, that by that time all the rest of the passengers behind you will be drowned—*like rats in a trap!* Good evening!"

"Wait!" Wentworth called sharply. "Wait, how long? Tell me how long before the explosion!"

The Red Hand laughed—and far off, rumbling, deep-toned, a detonation sent its echoes, then a hissing bomb of bursting air up past the train. Wentworth felt its jar strike against the car, rattle at its plates and sweep on. He heard, far off, a woman scream. And then, nothing—but the Red Hand's laughter!

Across the width of the train, Kirkpatrick stared into Wentworth's eyes. Neither man spoke but there was death in their eyes. Wentworth remained motionless, until he heard the clangor of a closing door, then he sprang to his feet and studied the air-tubes on the ceiling. He threw swift words at Kirkpatrick.

"I think one of these tubes may open the door when I put a bullet through it," he said. "There are blue lights marking emergency telephones. Get through to somebody important, if I succeed. Get them to back an empty train down from each side on the Manhattan-bound tubes. The Red Hand didn't say anything about that track. If the tracks are already short-circuited, they'll have to couple a series of trains together and not attempt to run them. Just back them down and use them as a walkway to safety. There are connections between the two tubes at intervals.

Then he threw a bullet through one of the air-tubes. There was a hiss of released air, the creaking of brakes letting go under the train, nothing more. Wentworth swore, picked another tube.

"I'm going to run back down and try to calm the people, start them walking to safety," he went on. "I don't know how big a hole they blew in the walls of the tube, but I don't believe it can be terribly big. The blast wasn't powerful enough. These tubes are tough."

He fired another shot, and nothing happened at all.

Kirkpatrick said gravely, "That sounds fine, Dick. But we won't get out of here. We...."

As Wentworth raised his gun to fire again, there came a distant hiss of air and the doors slid open. He heard someone running on the concrete walkway beside the tracks, the sharp tapping of a woman's heels. Instantly, Wentworth leaped out of the car, stared toward the back of the train. A woman was running toward him, staggering, pressing hands to her temples as she came.

A gasp came from Wentworth's throat, a name that he just choked down. God, he would know her anywhere, in any garb. Kirkpatrick was beside him now.

"A woman," he said sharply, "Did she let us out?"

"Spider!" The woman called in a queer strained voice. "Spider?"

Kirkpatrick gasped. "Nita van Sloan! I know that voice!"

NITA STUMBLED into Wentworth, gripped his arms. Her face was strained and white. "An explosion behind us there somewhere. I opened the doors as soon as I could. I jumped on the back of the train when it left Bowling Green station, but I couldn't do anything until it stopped. I…" She swayed weakly on her feet and Wentworth caught her. Behind him, he heard a voice say weakly, "Hey, what the hell?" Blaine was standing in the doorway.

"Take him with you, Kirkpatrick," Wentworth snapped. "And hurry, man. Hurry! Miss van Sloan, you go with…."

Nita straightened. "No," she said quietly. "That explosion. There'll be panic behind. I could see train after train slowing down behind us, and…."

"It's more than panic," Wentworth spoke swiftly, explaining. "For God's sake, hurry. All of you. Get to phones."

Nita's face was dead white. She shook her head. "No, my place is back there."

Wentworth's hands bit into her arms. He did not need her words to tell him what she meant. Her place was back there with

162

the man she loved. She could not say that before Kirkpatrick, lest she betray the Spider.

Kirkpatrick said quietly, "As soon as I get the calls made, I'll come back to you, Spider. Come, Blaine." He turned and began to run uphill toward where a blue light winked in the distance.

Blaine said, uncertainly, "I know something about operating these trains. I'll try to get her going again. By the lie of her she's off the track, but maybe…" He ran ahead.

Nita crept into Wentworth's arms. "Oh, Dick, *Dick!*" she whispered. "Why did you leave me? You know that if you go into danger, I go too!"

Wentworth laughed, starting back down-grade toward the river bottom, toward the death trap of the Red Hand. Nothing could beat him now. Nothing! He laughed again… and his laughter stilled. Already he could hear the screams and the shouts of panic. And he could hear another, more ominous thing. The roar and hiss of inrushing water!

They reached the rear of the train and Wentworth wrenched loose two lanterns, handed one to Nita and took one himself. Together, they jumped to the roadbed.

"Do you think you could sing, Nita?"

Nita's hand tightened on his arm. "With you, Dick, I can do anything!"

"All right, let's go. Something everybody will know. Try 'Pack Up Your Troubles in your Old Kit Bag'…."

Strangely clear and sweet, Nita's rich contralto lifted, and Wentworth joined her. Together, they marched down the middle of the tracks, singing. A man came pelting along the concrete walkway, shouting, beating the air with his fists, blind with panic. Behind him, a thin line of others. Their own terror was blockading the narrow path. People fought and scrambled and few succeeded in battling their way clear. The man in the lead saw Nita and Wentworth. His mouth stayed open on a shout, but the sound stopped. He still ran, but he was calmer. As he hurried past them, his head swung sideways toward the man and woman, who walked singing back to meet the doom he fled and, abruptly, he stopped, stood swaying there on the walkway.

"God," he whispered. "God I left *Flora!*"

He turned and hurried back toward the panic, toward the stalled train.

"Take it easy!" Wentworth called after him. "How about joining in the song?"

"Pack up your troubles in your old kit bag, and smile… smile… smile…."

They marched on, singing, and presently, the man's uncertain voice joined. Startled faces, amid that mêlée at the train doors, turned toward the sound of singing voices. The train was a bare hundred feet away, but by the time Nita and Wentworth were three-quarters of the way there, a few thin voices had picked up the air. Wentworth leaped to the walkway.

"You've got plenty of time!" he shouted at the people. "It's the trains behind you that are in danger. Walk quietly along this walkway. There are emergency exits two hundred yards ahead. You've got all the time in the world. Once you're past that next train, you're safe. Safe, I tell you. Walk quietly!"

IT WAS easier here. Wentworth jumped down to the roadbed again, got out cigarettes and offered Nita one.

The moment something like order descended on the crowd, Wentworth helped Nita over the deadly third rail and they crowded past the stationary train on the side opposite from the walk, plunging deeper into the tube, toward the rising waters. Wentworth set his jaw grimly.

"Thank God," he whispered, "that the water is coming in slowly. If only those trains would hurry on the other track! Kirkpatrick must be having trouble with the officials."

"Or else," Nita put in quietly, "the Red Hand cut the wires!"

Wentworth let out a single sharp oath. "That's it, of course! Kirk had to get up an emergency exit, find a phone…" His lips closed in a thin, harsh line. "It's up to us, Nita," he said softly. "Up to us. Try to sing, darling…."

Their voices made small thin noises above the rush of the wind and water. The walkway was completely blocked by a group of four or five men locked in a fierce struggle. Arms flew out. Feet struck. And behind them, people screamed and battled to get by. A few were leaping to the tracks. A shot over the heads of the fighters accomplished nothing. Wentworth fired low into the tangle. There was a scream and, leaning outward, the whole mêlée pitched to the roadway. There was a flash of fire, another scream, and after that silence. They had struck the third rail!

"Keep on the walkway!" Wentworth shouted. "If you touch those men, you'll be killed, too!"

HE HELPED Nita to step cautiously past the men and once more they stood calmly smoking together near the train.

A few were soothed by their calm, but not even the threat of Spider lead could still the panic here. A gray-headed woman was standing in the open front door of the train, looking down at them. The door was too high for her and Wentworth helped her down. She smiled.

"Do you think I could help?" she said. "I'll never be able to get out. Give me a cigarette and let me be nonchalant, too."

Wentworth laughed, lifted her to a seat on the edge of the walkway and with grave courtesy lighted a cigarette for her. She coughed over the first puff, tilted back her head to blow smoke straight upward.

"I've always wanted to smoke in a subway," she confided. "How'm I doing?"

In watching her, people forgot their fury. A man stopped beside her. "Come on, mother," he said, "I'll carry you."

The old woman got heavily to her feet. "I'll be a load, young man," she said. "I wish now I'd watched my diet a bit better. Stoop down. No, turn your back. I'm going to ride piggy-back for once in my life!"

Wentworth turned away, his eyes stinging, and led Nita once more down the dark slot beside the train toward the hell deeper beneath the river. The old woman was doing her valorous work well. Nita said, with a catch in her voice, "I hope, if I live to be that old, that I'm as brave as she."

"You won't live to be that old," Wentworth said harshly. "Nita, you must go back. Look…" They had reached the end of the train now and, suddenly, the lights went out below them.

166

"You know what that means," Wentworth said. "The water has reached that circuit. In a few more minutes...."

"In a few more minutes," Nita said softly, "you're going to succeed in scaring me. Come on, Dick." Nita ran ahead. She had a new song now....

"Who's afraid of the big, bad wolf,
The big, bad wolf—the big, bad wolf...?
Who's afraid...?"

Wentworth noticed abruptly that there was no longer the sound of rushing water and, direfully, he knew what that meant. The level in the tunnels had risen above the break through which the river poured. They had descended hundreds of feet along the gradual slope of the tube. The train ahead, or surely the one after that, would be at the bottom of the river, literally. It would be under water. And the people in it? God, there was no way of telling! Perhaps some had escaped. Perhaps panic had doomed them all....

The screams from the train ahead sounded strangely muffled. No footsteps beat along the walkway. Abruptly, Wentworth seized Nita's hand and sprinted. He understood now! That train ahead was sealed tight! Because of jammed mechanism, or the stupidity of the operators, the doors were still shut! Abruptly, Wentworth threw an arm about Nita and dragged her to a halt. There was a new glint where the lantern rays struck the right-of-way, a moving surface that refracted the light. Water! They were still twenty-five feet from the front of the train and the river was moving in!

CHAPTER 16
WHEN RATS LEAVE

THERE WAS no thought of turning back now. Wentworth lifted Nita to the walkway, vaulted up himself, and together they raced on along the narrow side lane. If the water was visible twenty-five feet from the front of the train, in the last car, it must be already reaching for the ceiling. God, there was no time, no *time*… Wentworth skidded to an abrupt halt.

"Run up to the next train," he cried to Nita. "Make the train-men run it back and hook on to this one, drag it clear. We can gain a few minutes that way!"

Nita raced back the way she had come. Wentworth ran on. Three cars from the back, the water was lapping over the walkway. At the back of the second car, people were waist deep in water. The third car… Their screams held the note of madness. Jammed into the front half of the coach where alone they could get their heads above water, the people were packed immovably together. Someone had begun a hymn and a few wavering voices bore up the melody. At a glance, Wentworth took in the picture by the faint rays of his lantern. Windows and doors had already been smashed out. A few had managed to squeeze through, but the openings were too small.

Wentworth thumbed the release buttons for the doors, but it was plain that had been done long ago. No air released. The doors did not move. He fought his way through the water which sucked and washed about his waist, creeping higher, higher with each passing second. He reached the first door. The doors were locked, he knew, by a jointed arm which elbowed upward when they slid back and, straightening, locked into position. If he could get at that elbow… But it operated between walls of steel. It just lifted into view, Wentworth remembered, at the window nearest the door. Water was chest-high when he reached the window. He smashed it out with a gun, groped downward through the dark water. At arm-length down between the steel walls, his fingers slid down on each side of the bar, but he could not get a grip. The space between the steel walls was too narrow!

"I need a strong man here!" Wentworth called. "Here at this window. Hurry!"

His hands had flown to his waist, were ripping off his belt. If he could loop that around under the elbow, then two of them could pull upward on it… He groped the belt down through the narrow slot. He had to bend over to reach deeply and it was then he realized how swiftly the water was rising. Previously, his face had not touched the water. Now he must hold his breath and plunge under to his ears!

The roiling roar of inrushing water came to him clearly with his ears underwater. He heard a man shouting nearby, but couldn't answer. His fingers fumbled with the belt. He had dropped the buckle end down on one side of the locking bar, was trying to hook a finger through on the opposite side. Twice he almost had it, then he was forced to straighten up for breath. He had hooked the lantern handle over a knob on the side of the car, and a man's face was thrust into the pool of light.

"Wait," Wentworth snapped at him. "Think I can open the door."

169

Once more he ducked under and this time, on the third try, he managed to finger the belt beneath the elbow and pass the tip through the buckle.

"Wait," he said once more. "If this belt breaks, we are lost. It must be a slow lift together…" Gripping the slippery leather in his fists, Wentworth strained upward. The man locked two fists upon his and added his strength. The elbow broke upward sharply, the doors parted. With a spring, Wentworth was at the door, hurling it back into its slot.

"Take charge!" he yelled at the man. "You've got time to get clear if you don't rush the door!"

In two movements, he freed his belt and raced on to the next car. Now that he had learned the way.…

WHEN WENTWORTH opened the fourth door, he was forced to dive and hold himself under water and those who escaped must dive and swim or pull themselves along beneath the surface. Nerve-breaking work. Many, rather than attempt it, clung to the front part of the car where alone they could breathe. Now that a way was opened, a few had regained their sanity. Wentworth set them the task of seizing these panic-trapped few and thrusting them underwater to safety. But the work could not long be continued. Scores would drown there.…

Wentworth raced to the next car and started smashing at the window glass with his gun. His hands were cut in a dozen places, numb from the deep-water cold in which he labored. And he knew this was futile. Before he could open this door, they would be trapped by the flood as other scores had been in the coach behind. He should leave them, go on to the next car where he might have a chance at rescue. He should... but he could not. As long as there was a chance to save one man's life....

A hand tapped him on the shoulder and Wentworth turned a harassed face. It was Don Blaine and no one else!

"That first train is hopeless for me alone," Blaine shouted above the panic tumult. "No chance to get it on the track single-handed. Tell me what to do here!"

Wentworth told him, gasping, while he labored on. Blaine started floundering ahead to open the next car and Wentworth stopped him.

"Bubbles is a real girl," Wentworth told him, "and she loves nobody but you. You were wrong to suspect her at Ransome's last night. I know. I was there."

Blaine stared at him, face yellow in the faint lantern glow. Suddenly, he grinned.

"Thanks, Spider!" he cried. He bounded to the work exultantly and there was a grim smile on Wentworth's lips as he went on with the rescue work. Those few seconds had not been wasted. Blaine would work twice as hard and fast for a happy heart....

Wentworth found that his lips were moving as he feverishly cleared the glass so that he could work the locking bar of this door. A prayer? Perhaps. A prayer of thankfulness for one man of altruism among all these who thought only of escape. Once more he pulled himself down beneath the water. People floundered past him. A swimmer's foot hit him glancingly on the skull, drove his face against the steel wall. Still, Wentworth clung on doggedly. His hands groped, strained with the belt. He could not be sure whether it was in place. The last feeling had gone from his hands. But he thought the belt was in place. He prayed to God it was! He popped to the surface, holding to the belt, braced his feet and strained upward and the door slid protestingly open.

"The door is open!" he shouted.

"You'll have to walk underwater. Hurry...."

There was a thin floundering and one, two men, one woman fought their way out of the door. That was all. The others had all—gone under. If there were the means, many of those might be saved; carried to dry land and resuscitated by artificial respiration. If there were the means—*and the time!*

WENTWORTH TURNED up the walkway, pulling himself along by the sides of the car until his feet hit bottom, then trying to walk. He fell twice. The second time, it was his bodily buoyancy more than his will which drew him to the surface again. He clung to the side of the coach, panting. The lantern... Oh, yes, he had given it to Blaine. Well, there was more work to do. The Spider... must go on. A wrenching jar ran through the train and it slipped backward a foot, two feet. God, was all his work for nothing? If the train rolled backward down the incline... Crazily, he seized hold of a window frame and braced his feet. As if he could hold back those tons of steel!— And then, then, incredibly, the train began to... *to move forward!*

It dragged Wentworth along by his arms. He laughed out loud. Of course. Nita. He had given her a job to do and, as always, it was done. He let go and slopped along through the shallowing water, laughing, shouting. He bumped into Blaine and a strong arm was thrown around his shoulders.

"You did it, Spider," Blaine said hoarsely. "You, by God, did it!"

But a new thought had struck Wentworth. These cars still must be forced, and behind this one… There was a rumbling roar. A wave ran over the black surface of the water and reached after them, washed about their knees. Wentworth's hands gripped Blaine's arm.

"The tube has caved in," he said. He tried to shout, but it was a whisper. The roof had caved in, and now the water spurted after them as rapidly as they walked. Now it seemed to keep grim pace with Wentworth as he surged exhaustedly forward, a fate that could not be outrun, a doom that could not be evaded.

"Only one chance," Wentworth whispered. "Only one. If they'll send trains down the other track."

And then suddenly Nita was beside him with a flashlight, shouting that they were moving the trains up one at a time against the wrecked train, a gain of a few feet, a few minutes.

"Get to the train ahead, Blaine," he ordered hoarsely and the man was off.

"Good girl, Nita," Wentworth muttered, and sprung another door.

The rush of people swept him along for ten feet before he could catch himself. He clung to the side of the coach while frantic refugees battered past. Nita set her frail body as a shield for him. He threw an arm about her.

"Got to run these trains up," Wentworth said heavily. "Lots of those people in the back cars can be revived, if they'll only hurry. *Hurry!*" He fumbled his way into the motorman's compartment of the train, inched on power. The train ahead was crawling forward. Crawling… but they would have to go faster than that. The river….

Suddenly, a line of men in uniform was bounding past him, police and firemen coming to the rescue. A puff of air fanned his face, became a rushing blast that was swallowed in the hum of motors and clatter of running trains—on the other tracks! At last, Kirkpatrick had succeeded in getting action! Rescue trains were being backed down the unobstructed tracks, the Manhattan-bound rails. In a few moments now, people could be lifted through the connections that opened between the two tubes. There would be ample walkways to freedom now, space to work… Wentworth slumped back against the wall and smiled at Nita. She stepped close and threw her arms around him.

"WE MUST hurry, Dick," she whispered. "Hurry. When Kirkpatrick comes back with the police…."

Wentworth shook his head. "We must find Kirkpatrick. There's something the Red Hand said while we were there in the train when we were his prisoners. I had the solution, almost. And now, I can't think. I can't think. It was something to do with Blaine."

Nita urged him to his feet. "I was with Blaine for hours last night," she said. "He was drunk and he talked a lot. Perhaps… But let's walk out of here, Dick. The water is very close… I'll tell you what Blaine told me, part of it."

She told him then of Blaine's fears about Bubbles Morval, and his talk of marrying his boss.

"That would be Clare Sutton," Wentworth broke in. "I'm beginning to remember now. The Red Hand seemed to bear especial animosity toward Blaine and tried to cover it up afterward. Said something about Blaine falling in love with his secretary...."

"Ransome!" Nita cried. "Then it was Ransome all the time."

Wentworth frowned. "Tell me some more of what Blaine said."

"He said one thing that puzzled me," Nita said, more slowly. "He said that he couldn't marry his boss until the Red Hand was caught."

Wentworth stopped dead on the walkway—and had to step aside for a man to run past with a limp body on his shoulders. Everywhere the rescue was rushing forward now. Dozens of men, police and firemen, were charging past at a dead run. Wentworth slapped a fist into his palm. "That's it, by God! Nita, we've got to get to Ransome right away! No time to be lost... Hurry!"

He started to run along the walkway. He was sobbing for breath when he reached the exit stairway and began to fight his way upward. He had long ago lost his hat. His cape clung wetly to his body, but his makeup itself was waterproof. His face was still the face of the Spider—if anyone should identify it. But not one in a thousand could identify him by his face....

On the surface at long last, he strode to the nearest policeman. "Where is Kirkpatrick?" he demanded sharply.

"Down below, sir," the officer said. "May be able to reach him by telephone." He turned to a field station, set up near at hand. Trust Kirkpatrick to make sure of contact with all points! But it took time, and time was so infinitely important now. A fireman came up the emergency stairway with a man across his shoulder, a man who still was protesting in a weak voice. The fireman dumped him with a grunt.

"Damn fool almost got himself drowned doing rescues," the fireman growled. "Didn't want to stop."

Wentworth smiled at Blaine, dropped a hand on his shoulder. "It's all right, old man," he said. "There are plenty down below now to take over...."

Blaine stared at him, threw a quick look over his shoulder. "I knew that, sir, but I thought you were still down below, and I couldn't... couldn't... Damn it, sir, I know the police are after you hot and heavy, but you're a man, sir. A wonderful man!"

Wentworth laughed, "Spare my blushes, Blaine. After all...."

It was a whirlwind that swept past him, a small feminine whirlwind who flung her arms about Blaine's neck.

"Oh, Donald, Donald!" she cried. It was Bubbles Morval.

Blaine's arms closed around her weakly. "I want you to forgive me, Bubbles," he said awkwardly. "About last night, you know, I was a damned fool, and...."

"You can't help being a damned fool," Bubbles told him, with the bright, angry way she had. "Maybe that's why I love you so. I almost killed myself trying to get you out of that tunnel—from the other side! I was there on the platform, you know, when the Red Hand's train came through. When I saw you take that header inside, I called the cops. They were there when that explosion came and got right to work saving people. But we couldn't find you, darling. I finally heard about this rescue station here and took a taxi over… And here you were. Tell me, handsome, have I got to spend the rest of my life looking after you?"

Blaine laughed, deep in his chest. "Sure, honey. Sure!"

Wentworth drew Nita away, his arm about her waist. "Guess the Spider is some little matchmaker," he whispered.

"Punk," Nita grinned up at him. "He can't even catch a wife himself."

Wentworth turned away, hiding the pain that twisted his lips. Love for the Spider? When it could bring only pain and peril to those he loved? It was mockery; a travesty on tenderness. He was glad that the call to Kirkpatrick went through just then.

"Kirkpatrick, I know what the Red Hand is," Wentworth said, without preliminary. "I want orders to arrest Ransome and Sutton at once."

Kirkpatrick's voice cracked harshly. "No time for that now. There are hundreds still in danger…."

"And hundreds more will die if we don't get the Red Hand!" Wentworth hurled back at him. "There's not a moment to lose. Come up."

Kirkpatrick's chuckle was dry. "Sorry to disagree. I'll give the order to headquarters. I can reach them by phone. What you mean, I gather, is a special broadcast alarm to find Sutton and Ransome at all costs. We've already got out a quiet search for them now, you know."

"I know."

Kirkpatrick laughed. "I hope you can support your charges, Spider, or they'll be apt to sue you for false arrest! Incidentally, I've cancelled orders for Nita's and Wentworth's arrest."

Wentworth laughed, but there was no mirth in him. He sensed Kirkpatrick's relief, his joy at Wentworth's escape from the deathtrap in the tube. Nita caught at his arm.

"You know who the Red Hand is!" she whispered.

Wentworth shook his head. "Not *who* he is," he said quietly, "but *what* he is. Come, we must hurry!" He ran for a taxi and sent it racing for the bridge, for Manhattan.

"I don't understand," Nita cried above the rush of the wind.

"I don't entirely," Wentworth shouted back, "but the Red Hand is... *Clare Sutton's husband!*"

CHAPTER 17
THE SPIDER DIES

NITA STARED at Wentworth with widening eyes. "I don't understand," she said slowly. "You say the Red Hand is Clare Sutton's husband? Do you mean that Ransome is her husband? All your evidence has pointed to him. Certainly, Randolph Sutton isn't her husband. Everyone knows he's really Clare's father."

Wentworth shook his head. "No suspicion attaches to Sutton," he told her, "but we've got to get hold of him quickly, or he'll be killed... by the Red Hand!"

It was obvious, of course. Sutton was ultimately doomed, because until he died Clare would not inherit his money. And on Sutton's death, his estate would be found many millions richer than had been expected—the Red Hand would have ordered all the loot, all the proceeds of those many market coups he had planned, turned over to Sutton. It had to be that way. Nothing else fitted in to what he knew.

Subconsciously, Wentworth had been worried ever since this battle began over one thing: the manner in which the Red Hand could get hold of the money and still remain unidentified. Money paid over by brokers and criminals under fear of the Red Hand was sure to be traced eventually. But if it were paid to Sutton—and Sutton were innocent? Probably he could be proved innocent of any connection with the crimes. And then, if Sutton… died. His daughter, and *his daughter's husband*, would inherit it. And the Red Hand's statement in the trap car, his resentment at Blaine, taken with Clare's statement that before she could marry Blaine, the Red Hand must be caught… Yes, they meant one thing clearly—that the Red Hand was Clare Sutton's husband.

That would tie in, too, with his early discovery that Clare had been beaten. Somehow, she had got wind of what impended and had gone to Laskar to ask the Spider's help. And the Red Hand had beaten, not killed her, because she had to live so that he could get the money! Yes, it all fitted—but who was Clare Sutton's husband? Wentworth explained these things rapidly to Nita, then switched on the radio to hunt for a news broadcast.

The commentator was crying out against the Red Hand, but there were comparatively few disasters. The subway wreck and the fire on the elevated; the flooding of the tubes; one other fire on the elevated far uptown which had been almost abortive. The Red Hand would not consider it successful either. Four out of twenty-eight plotted disasters had been accomplished, and two of those were almost failures. True, the dead in the flooding of the tube would probably run over a hundred, but thousands had been saved. That was not in accordance with the Red Hand's plan. And he would not be able to cash in on it tomorrow, for Kirkpatrick had notified every Wall Street trader that there would be no trading in subway or elevated stocks for a week; that any man attempting so to trade would be instantly arrested. The news commentator was detailing this at great length now. It had been a shrewd move. It meant the Red Hand's work was at a standstill. He could recoup his forces, reorganize, but if the Spider could strike now….

Wentworth found himself sitting on the edge of his seat, urging the taxi driver to greater and greater speed.

"Nita," he said, "you must go to your home. Get things ready for me to make a quick change when I come there."

Nita stared at him with widening eyes. "I don't understand, Dick," she whispered.

"I'm going up against the police and the Red Hand," he said curtly. "It's probable I'll have to make a run for it. If I can get three minutes' leeway, I'll come to you… then let them look for me!"

Nita leaned toward him, her hand gripped on his. "Dick," she said. "Promise me. Promise me…."

Wentworth kissed her gently. "Within an hour, you'll see me again, darling. I promise you! Now, hurry…."

He stopped the cab and Nita jumped out, stood on the corner as long as Wentworth's cab remained in sight, her hand lifted in farewell. She paid no attention to the curious stares that were turned on her and there was a sob in her throat as she stumbled toward another taxi. Dick had promised, and if he were alive, he would keep that promise, but always he must plunge into deadly peril. The Red Hand and the police… She suspected that he had only found an excuse to put her out of danger's way.…

UNDER WENTWORTH'S urging, the cab was racing through traffic, weaving a perilous course, bound for Ransome's home. The police should be there ahead of him, but their orders were only to arrest Ransome, and the Spider knew they would fail in that. The Red Hand was either in flight, or he was preparing to cover his trail for a new start. He had no alternatives… Wentworth flung money at the driver, darted into the service entrance of the building. Precious seconds were wasted picking the lock, other seconds waiting for the automatic elevator, but at last he was moving upward. Tautly, he stepped back and forth across the narrow cage of the elevator. If he were too late.…

He jerked open the doors, sprang to the service entrance of the apartment. Police might be, probably were, inside but he must risk that. He worked quietly now with the lock pick and, moments later, was slipping inside. The apartment held a waiting silence and through it, Wentworth stole toward the drawing room… His hand was on the door when a shot crashed out beyond the panel, echoing a man's choked scream. Wentworth's gun sprang to his hand. He batted open the door, stood transfixed.…

A single light burned in the drawing room, a bridge lamp with a powerful bulb whose shade focused its white rays downward. They spilled across a man dying in a chair, a man with a bullet hole through his forehead and with another crimson stain there that was not blood… Dazedly, Wentworth recognized that symbol. It was his own! It was the seal of the Spider!

This would give the police a problem all right. The man in the chair, dead, under the seal of the Spider, was Ransome. He had come too late to save the lawyer. And that figure fleeing across the room wore the black cape and hat of the Spider! When the police found both men dead, both men marked with the seal… His automatic's hammer clicked forward, and that was all! Long immersion had ruined his ammunition. Across the room, the man in the cape and hat of the Spider was chuckling, a laughter whose tone Wentworth well knew—*The Red Hand!*

Then flame lanced across the room and Wentworth went down, hammered back against the swing door, driven into the kitchen by the hellish shock of lead. He did not feel himself strike the floor, but knew presently that he was there flat on his back, a hand pressed to the agony in his side. Distantly, he heard a door clap shut. He thrust himself to his feet, reeled to the service door, to the elevator. Heaven knew why the police had delayed so long, but they could not be long in arriving. By God, the Red Hand had planned well! Nothing would convict Ransome so surely as the Spider's seal on his brow, for the Spider never yet had slain an innocent man.

Moreover, the Red Hand had taken pains to wear the cape and hat of the Spider, so he would allow himself to be seen in his flight from the building. That would put the final seal upon the evidence, unless… unless Wentworth could trap the man and kill him in his habiliments. Something like bitter laughter strained in Wentworth's throat. Kill an armed man when he himself was wounded and his guns useless....

Through the service hallway to the street, he reeled, found his taxi still waiting. He stumbled into it.

"Around the corner, quickly!"

The cab rolled and, as they whirled the corner, a man in the Spider's cape sprang out under the lighted canopy of the building and into a waiting coupé; drove it swiftly away while building attendants stood in the doorway and shrieked. Yes, the Red Hand had given ample proof all right. He... As the coupé whirled into a cross-cut through Central Park, police sirens were abruptly whining all around Wentworth. A radio prowl car whirled into the cross-cut behind the Red Hand; two more crowded past Wentworth's taxi.

WENTWORTH SETTLED back on the cushions. "Keep in sight of that coupé!" he ordered. Methodically, then, he pulled aside coat and vest to inspect the wound in his side. It could not be too serious or he never would have traveled so far unaided. With flinching fingers, he explored the wound, leaned back faint with pain. A long gutter had been drilled along his right side. The rib was broken, but he thought no other more serious injury had been done. Presently, as the pain diminished, he was stronger. He leaned forward to watch the chase, cursing his empty guns.

Just as the coupé darted out of the westward end of the cross-cut, flame slashed out of its rear window and the leading prowl car turned broadside, skated across traffic and slammed into a truck head-on. The other two cars raced on, and Wentworth urged the taxi to greater speed.

"Not me, boss," the driver said. "I'll keep him in sight like you said, but I ain't getting in the way of no bullets. Didn't you see who that guy was? It's the Spider!"

Wentworth frowned over the reply. It meant that police murder would be laid at the Spider's door, unless… unless the Red Hand could be trapped in the robes of the Spider. The chase was bearing due westward now. With a start, Wentworth realized that if the Red Hand kept on he would come out on Riverside Drive within a half block of Nita's apartment house. The devil! Was the Red Hand carrying his impersonation so far.…

Grimly, Wentworth recognized that the Red Hand was bent not only on laying the blame for Ransome's death on the Spider and thus sealing the evidence, but that he was also bent on vengeance. He could not be wrong. The Red Hand had sped too straight to this spot for it to be accidental. And Wentworth could not get there first.

When Wentworth's taxi turned the corner into Riverside Drive, the two police cars and the coupé were stationary before Riverside Towers, where Nita lived. And the police were all in sight. They were blockading the building while one of them shouted to the doorman to call police headquarters for reinforcements.

"We got the Spider trapped in this building!"

They had the Spider trapped, and up there Nita was waiting for him to come, waiting for Wentworth to rush in and assume a disguise that would fool the police! If she heard that shout, she would go to meet this false Spider, and find… what? Would the Red Hand know that she had foiled his under-river massacre? Would he use her to make good his escape—or would he take his vengeance even in the face of the police?

Furiously, Wentworth flung himself at the door of the building next to the Riverside Towers. His guns were useless, but the elevator operator could not know that.

"Top floor," Wentworth ordered hoarsely. "And hurry, damn you!"

The elevator shot him upward and he ran for the stairs to the roof, burst out. As he remembered, the fire escape from the Towers descended by retractable ladder to this roof. He ran to it, sprang upward, and felt pain stab through his side as bleeding started afresh. But he made the ladder and clung while it slid downward. Moments later, he was fighting his way up the ladder. But when he confronted the Red Hand with useless guns….

More siren noise was filling the streets now as more and more police cars skidded into Riverside Drive. The street was jamming with them. Searchlights threw their broad purple beams over the front of the Towers, raked its side so that the shadow of the fire escape sprang up black and bold across the building.

He heard a man shout and a machine gun began to burn slugs past him as he climbed. They rang on the steel latticework, gouged out brick dust from the wall, but the steel protected Wentworth and he kept it ever between him and that gun. Nita was on the fifteenth floor. Already he had risen twelve above the street. This fire escape went under her kitchen window….

He was on the fourteenth floor when, just overhead, a gun

185

hammered out inside. Violently, Wentworth flung himself at the steps upward, saw a man leap out of the window of Nita's apartment and race upward. And the Spider's guns were useless. He was sobbing with rage as he flung upward. Those shots in Nita's apartment, what did they mean? God, the Red Hand could not... could not....

AT THE window of Nita's apartment, Wentworth stood for a long moment and, through the kitchen door, Nita came slowly. She was holding her head, staggering, but there was a gun in her right hand.

"Nita!" Wentworth called softly. "Throw me your gun!"

Nita uttered a glad cry. "Dick, Oh, thank God! Come in. Everything is ready for you...."

Wentworth hesitated there on the window sill, on the brink of safety. He could spring inside and within minutes could transform himself into his own identity. Up there on the roof, the Red Hand crouched and waited for the police....

"Give me your gun, Nita," Wentworth said again.

For a moment she hesitated, then silently, white-faced, she gave him the gun. Tears welled in her eyes, made their tracery down her cheeks.

"The Red Hand must have some way of escaping from the building, Nita," Wentworth said swiftly. "Otherwise, he never would have come here like this. I'm afraid he may fool the police."

Nita clasped his face in her hands and kissed him on the mouth. Wentworth tore himself away and hurried up the parapet and threw himself prone.

Gunflame lanced at him from behind a dumbwaiter shaft head and Wentworth threw lead from Nita's gun.

"Come out and fight, Red Hand," Wentworth called, and laughed. "It is the Spider come for you!"

He heard the Red Hand curse viciously and three swift shots pumped lead at the spot where Wentworth lay. Wentworth fired once more at the flashes, squeezed the trigger again… and the gun was empty. He sprang to his feet, darted toward the kiosk behind which the Red Hand crouched, heard the man's curses, the clicking mechanical sounds of reloading—and Wentworth laughed! Laughed, while he charged unarmed upon the Red Hand, a wounded Spider going into battle.

"Too late, Red Hand!" he called. "Too late. I'm coming for you!"

He swiveled around the corner of the kiosk and dodged under a sweeping blow. His shoulder caught the man in the chest and hurled him backward. The Red Hand fell, rose drunkenly. There was a glint of metal in that right hand and for a moment, Wentworth thought it was a gun he held. Then, with a chill of horror, he recognized the thing for what it was—the fearful steel gauntlet of the Red Hand!

"Come on, Spider," the Red Hand's voice reached him in a whisper. "Come on, I've been longing to give you a *taste* of this!"

Wentworth laughed again—and charged.

BUT IT was no blind leap. He went racing in, checked at the last moment. The steel hand swept past his face with only inches to spare, and Wentworth swayed forward at the same instant. His left hand gripped the Red Hand's right arm above the elbow, closing excruciatingly on certain nerve centers there. His right hand fastened on the wrist of that steel gauntlet and behind the thrust of those two hands went the weight and impetus of his charge. The Red Hand cried out and stumbled backward, went down screaming under the blow of Wentworth's body.

The Spider's aim was not at its best. He had meant that steel gauntlet to strike the face of the Red Hand. It took him on the throat instead. For a while, the man screamed terribly, and for a while after, there were only groans. When Wentworth got dizzily to his feet, there was no sound and no movement at all—and the fingers of the steel glove had met in the throat of the Red Hand.

Wentworth bent over him, planting the base of his gleaming cigarette holder on the broad intelligent forehead. This would be Clare Sutton's husband all right, but she would not marry Blaine, though widowed. The scene at the emergency exit of the subway, Bubbles close in Blaine's arms, resolved that. And he had guessed right. When he had deduced that the Red Hand would be the husband of Clare Sutton, his mind had flashed back to the fact he had mentioned in Kirkpatrick's office, that Clare had gone for months with the racketeer, Michael Taug, and then suddenly ceased. She had stopped after Taug had got what he wanted, their marriage. Thereafter, it would be best for them to separate. The Red Hand… in the Spider's robes, dead under the Spider's seal. Tomorrow, he would explain these things to Kirkpatrick.

Suddenly, Wentworth laughed. He bent over the body of Michael Taug and lifted it easily to his shoulder. Presently, the police climbing the fire escape, saw a caped figure standing on the balustrade.

"You'll never take the Spider alive!"

It was a clear black silhouette against the glow of the night sky, a perfect target. A machine gun blasted below and up there on the roof, a man screamed terribly—and the black figure of the Spider toppled downward, struck the roof.

Far above them, Wentworth laughed softly. Let them puzzle over the enigma of the Spider dead, wearing the Red Hand's gauntlet and the Spider's seal on his brow. It would not fool the police long. Kirkpatrick, when he came, would understand that this dead man was the Red Hand, slain by the Spider; that once more the Spider had escaped a perfect police trap, this time by pretending he had been killed! But by that time, Blinky McQuade would be asleep in his room far down on the East Side.

And Nita? Death and torture had been too close to his beloved. He turned away from the window where Nita's love waited....

Once more, the Spider vanished.